"The Messiah?"

This is not the story you think you know...

By A.B. Naas

As Told to Woodrow Manning Jr.
Volume 1

For information contact: info@uptownmediaventures.com

Book and Cover design by Team Uptown

ISBN: 978-1-68121-015-5

First Edition: April 2015

This book is dedicated to my grandson Umar. May he never forget the past that is the foundation of his present and future.

Page left intentionally blank

Acknowledgements

First and foremost I thank the GOD of my understanding. I would like to thank the editors that have labored so hard to make this a book easy to read. I also thank the publisher who has given me the opportunity to share this story. A special thanks to my friend Imam Shaheed for being my brother for forty plus years. Last but not least I would like to thank my wife of thirty-nine years. Without her none of this would have been possible.

Page left intentionally blank

Chapters   Page

Prologue

I DECLARE THAT THESE ARE THE CHRONICLES OF A.B. NAAS! I FURTHER DECLARE THAT I AM A.B. NAAS!

Of course you will ask, "Who am I to make such a declaration? And now that such a declaration has been made what comes of it?" I will answer your second question first, in so far as who I am is not the issue in these pages you are about to read. But we will get to all things that the time and space we have allows.

Yes, time! Space - we will get to that too, in time. My Chronicles are a journey around the circle of time. Yes, I know, time can be many things. From the perspective of these Chronicles, time is best viewed as a circle. 'Why is it?' you ask. Is it not true that before the time you speak of there is not a before? Is it not also true that after the time you finish there is more or let us possibly suggests another time? So where does a circle begin or end? Does it matter? Should it matter? Yes I know questions and pointless riddles, perhaps?

Why has A.B. Naas decided to add to the space of already too many words that people ignore or have no interest? Let's say it seemed like a good idea at the time. Some who read these words know all too well the dangers that lie in the universe of the mind. Sometimes the reverberation of a thought echo back as a good one to pursue. In the space that I fill with these words one such a thought did I so pursue.

Everything that is important to me is of no use to you. Everything you need to know about me, you already have been told. I simply add to further clarify that I am the man, if it be a man - that I am behind the curtain. The history, that is not important. The man you have been told to ignore, don't listen to, or overlook. However, you can no more overlook me than you can overlook your own image in a mirror. I have always been there and right here as you shall always be! Yes, I am A.B. NAAS and this I do declare and proclaim!

These Chronicles are a journey and it does not matter where we start. Let me caution you, you may not like what you see. Are these Chronicles fact or fiction? Is it possible for them to be neither or both? We know and are all familiar with the so-called facts that are false. Words that are said or written that are not true and can be proven as such. I mean to further clarify. Have you ever considered that maybe; just maybe there are false facts that are true?

This is my promise, I will not tell you what to think or believe. As for what I believe it is or will be of no use to you. All that I show you through my eyes if these are eyes through which I see. Will it be only that which is there, or possibly their? Whichever it is you will soon discover if, and only if, you decided to take this journey with me? For one so bold dare I say, one so brave? This promise will be my oath and to it shall I be true. I say this and I swear by ALL THAT I AM ALLOWED TO SWEAR BY! Yes I too have rules and guidelines I must follow. If only it were not so. Not a dream or an aspiration just a thought that I share. For in these Chronicles from time to time my thoughts too, do I share.

If it is not clear by now that in these Chronicles there is much to consider then I have failed. You should stop reading and go do what you would be doing otherwise. If I have been successful in this introduction then I promise you that everything and I mean everything will look just a little different once you have traveled with me.

I DECLARE THAT I AM A.B. NAAS AND THESE ARE MY CHRONICLES!"

Introduction

This is not "The Beginning" you are looking for. The preceding sentence will not make sense until you are looking for "The Beginning." So for now, if you are looking for "The Beginning" you will know what to do. If you are not looking for "The Beginning" I encourage you to keep reading. What follows is a very interesting story. Sooner or later you will get to the point where you have to come back. When you come back to this page looking for "The Beginning," you too will know what to do.

I am Woodrow Manning Jr. A name in my present time that is rarely if ever given to a newborn child (some would say for good reason). However, for me it is a name that is quite fitting. Besides the fact that the name honors my father, it is also historically significant. The name speaks in a way to my lifelong love of history.

Perhaps my affinity for history began with a gift of a book? The book was entitled, *A Coat of Many Colors*. It was given to me on my fifth birthday by my beloved cousin Ida Mae Wise Anderson. The book told the story of Joseph, son of Jacob. I was captivated by the story and it made me thirsty for more. It was not hard to find more stories. I found many more stories in a book called *The Bible*.

I can't say for sure when exactly I met A.B. Naas. As I look back over my life I can remember seeing glimpses of him periodically. We were never formally introduced. He just showed up. At first he was just there. I mostly ignored him. I was busy; I had places to go, people to see and thing to do. It was not until I came face to face with my mortality and physical limitations that I began to listen. It turns out that he had a lot to say. Most of it was extremely interesting. One thing I can say for a fact, he has never bored me.

As I listened I learned, not so much from what he had to say. Not to trivialize his words but these were just words. I learned from what he pointed out without saying a word. Don't get me wrong his words were and can be a source of great knowledge, wisdom and information. However, relative to the things that he pointed out. His words are the equivalent of a snowflake on the tip of an iceberg.

I can't really say for sure how much time I have spent listening to him. Come to think of it, the question itself is meaningless. I do not know when it was that I last spoke to him. If I were to say it has been a while since we last spoke. And also say with the same breath, I spoke to him just a moment ago and that both answers would be true and not in conflict.

Not too long ago I asked if I could put his words in writing. He thought for a moment (maybe it was for a long time) and then said "yes," but under one condition. The condition is that I would only write what he had to say exactly as he said it. I agreed. So, here you have it. The Chronicles of A.B. Naas as told to Woodrow Manning Jr.

In closing, I will say you are welcome in advance.

W.M. Jr.

Foreword

(briefly)

You do not have to go far to begin to understand Zadok's story. However, you have to get to Fars to understand both the time and space that covers the time and space of his story. Once you reach Fars from that point on you will know to place close attention to everything you read.

Chapter 1

The "Messiah" Is Dead?

"The Messiah is dead." The statement from the banker had all of the finality of a yes or no answer to a question of, "Is there a cloud in the sky?" The merchant from Hebron whose name was Eber with a tone clearly to question without challenging sheepishly stated, "There are those who still claim that they have seen him in the area of Galilee."

"No, the Romans Crucified him I saw it myself and I should know. That Messiah attacked me at the Temple not more than a year ago, it was him I say, I saw him on the cross," spat the banker. The banker's tone was clear to everyone that he was not to be challenged on this issue.

The time was late and though it was not customary to linger after the meal. For some reason tonight it seemed appropriate. The merchants and bankers had all assembled at the home of Tobiad. Tobiad was the richest and most respected Ehudi banker in all of Palestine. All present were more than a bit uneasy about the movement began by the so-called "Messiah." Zadok had begun to think of him as a so-called "Messiah." There had been many claimants to the title of "Messiah." But this one, this Joshua was different in many ways. He could do things that no man could explain or do.

Before the declaration of the banker that the "Messiah" is dead, there had been much discussion about this Joshua. Joshua, yes Joshua was his name. Some say he could heal the lame, cure the lepers and even raise the dead! By whatever name that he would be called, the elite among the Tribes of Israel were more than a little uneasy about the multitudes of the poor and common folks that flocked to his movement. It even became an issue for the Romans when this Joshua challenged their appointed high priest of the Temple of Solomon.

Everyone in the dinner circle spoke Hebrew but, their accents at times were a bit difficult for young Zadok to understand. In addition to Hebrew he spoke Aramaic (both east and west), and the languages of the Axum People and that of the Children of Ishmael. His grandfather was the Chief priest among priests of the Children of Israel, in all of the Province of Fars in the land of the Parthians. His grandfather had taught him many things and young Zadok had hoped to learn many more from this great man. However, his grandfather would not, could not, in good conscience teach him the language of the People of Darkness. This language that now contaminated the Hebrew spoken of those present.

The conversation ended with a joke from the Greek Tax Collector asking the question, "I wonder did he pay his taxes before they nailed him to that cross?" Everyone except Zadok and his father Aaron laughed, collected themselves, and departed.

What was most surprising to young Zadok was that in addition to the customary Shalom, many of the fifteen or so men that were present also said, "Hail Caesar!" This was quite surprising to young Zadok. Hail to the King of the People of Darkness! Whatever, the word "hail" meant he did not know. He believed that he heard it just once before. It was used by his grandfather as he recalls. It was not a good word and he was told never to repeat it by his grandmother. To say the King of Darkness' name in the same breath as Shalom was a curious thing indeed!

Young Zadok had been taught by his grandfather to have no love at all for the Romans. To him they were a barbaric people with no respect for anything but, their lust for all things material and sensual. His grandfather believed that the stolen Greek culture the Romans claimed was even more detestable. Aaron anticipated his son's aversions and instructed him to suppress his feelings.

As young Zadok walked behind his father and his Great Uncle Caleb his head was spinning. If the "Messiah" was dead then he had come too late. His Mission of Discovery was a failure. However, if the "Messiah" was truly the "Messiah" how could he possibly be dead? Do not all men die? Would not even the "Messiah" die? These were too many thoughts and too many questions for such a late hour. Zadok was physically, mentally, and possibly even spiritually exhausted. It had been three days since they had arrived in the City of David. The City of David was not at all what he had expected.

Zadok remembered he had his prayers still to say. By the time that they had reached his Great Uncle's modest villa. Zadok was so exhausted that he barely remembered saying his prayers and preparing for rest. He fell asleep the moment his head touched the pillow.

Lessons Learned From Grandfather Joshua
(Did he say hail or hell?)

Zadok had heard the adults speak of the priest Enoch who was sent to Fars by the High Priest at the Temple of Solomon in the City of David. The priest Enoch was from the Tribe of Levi. It was the custom of the Children of Israel to concede the role of priest to a member so trained from the Tribe of Levi. The priest Enoch arrived in Fars and the village to assume his rightful place. Zadok's grandfather thought different. His grandfather grabbed the priest by the beard and physically threw him out of the Village Temple.

"Where was the Tribe of Levi when my ancestors were carried off as slaves?" grandfather shouted! "You, the Tribe of Levi, and all the other Tribes can go to Hell! If you need help getting there let me see your face here again!" Not one of the village Elders or members said a word to grandfather about his action. They behaved for the rest of the day as if it never happened. (It would be many years before Zadok would understand why).

Later that same day as Zadok was tucked into bed by his Grandmother she said, "Zadok." "Yes, Grandmother," he responded very tired from an extremely confusing day. "Your grandfather was very angry today and he used a word that I want you to promise me you will never repeat. Now promise me you will never repeat that word," his Grandmother said in her most demanding and gentle voice. Zadok was earlier shocked by his grandfather's actions more than anything. While he thought he remembered the word, he was looking for confirmation. He hoped that he could get his Grandmother to repeat the word. He questioned, "What word Grandmother?"

He would later recall fondly that she saw right through his intent. She said with a smile, "It is good that you did not remember the word. But when you do, promise me you will not say it again." Zadok said, "I promise." She kissed him on his forehead and said, "Good, now get some rest. Your lessons begin right after the morning prayers. Grandfather and I love you very much Zadok." "I love you too," Zadok says as he drifted off to sleep.

Zadok Remembers hearing the word "hail" for the first time. That was ten years ago. He was six years old at the time.

Chapter 2

Words

(Thoughts Of A.B. Naas)

While young Zadok sleeps, I thought that here would be a convenient place to let you know that from time to time it will be necessary to share my thoughts with you. You see I have not forgotten my promise. You don't remember my promise? How soon do we forget so many things of importance? However, I have not forgotten.

Speech is considered by some to be the lowest form of communication. Then what does that make writing when we have to reduce our thoughts to a written word? How does one then communicate without betraying one's oath and or revealing one's beliefs? For example, if I were to use the word "fate" would that not mean that my belief systems sprang from a foundation based somewhere in or around Greece? On the other hand, to use the world "destiny" could mean that my belief system was based on a foundation of a belief system almost anywhere else?

Woodrow Manning Jr.

Both questions assume that to begin with, I would know the difference. No answers, just wanted you to know that I have considered my words carefully. Maybe you should remember that words do have meanings - don't they?

Now let's join Zadok. He is about to be awaken for the Morning Prayer.

Chapter 3

The City of David

During his stay in The City of David Zadok had pledged to make every Morning Prayer at the Temple of Solomon. He did not fully appreciate that his Great Uncle's Villa was actually a fair distance from the Temple. So, every morning he would awaken in enough time to walk to the Temple for the congregational prayer.

This was not the City of David he expected. The City he expected was the City of David of Mighty King Solomon! That was the City of David handed down from one generation to another by his people in the Province of Fars. As young Zadok walked to the Temple he no longer thought of it as the Temple of Solomon. He thought instead of that ancient longed vanished Temple build by the Mighty King Solomon. He knew that to think of that City of David during the time of Solomon would quicken his step. It would provide him the energy he needed to overcome the cries of his body craving more rest.

It was only natural for his people to pass on to Zadok, the image of the City of David under Mighty King Solomon. That was the City of David that they knew before the Assyrians took them away in bondage. That was a very hard time for the Tribe of Joseph. It was said by some that this was a punishment. It was also said that the Assyrians had received help. This help came from some of the other Tribes among the Children of Israel. This thought young Zadok quickly put out of his mind because it so depressed him. But still the thought lingered there in the background waiting for another opportunity to present itself.

Mighty King Solomon! Son of King David! Of the Children of Israel, in the stories of his people, King Solomon was the most powerful man who had ever lived! Some would go so far as to say he would be the mightiest man to ever live! When such statements were made in the presence of his grandfather, Zadok would look at him immediately. His grandfather had no patience at all for grand boasts of any kind. His grandfather would just smile, paying no attention to anyone as he looked off into the distance. On a few occasions young Zadok thought that the eyes of his grandfather would grow glassy. Young Zadok was still too young to understand the yearning for things lost. Young

Zadok had never lost anyone or anything close to him. Unfortunately, given time, this would change.

Zadok day dreamed more about the City of David and of Mighty King Solomon as he drew ever closer to the Temple of his disappointment.

The Young Roman Soldier

Lost in thought, Zadok was unaware of how close he was now walking to the shadows cast by the lack of torch light on the street. He was startled when out of the darkness emerged a figure not quite discernible in the shadows. Zadok reacted as he was expected to from his training. He swung his staff and stopped just short of his target as what he now saw was a young Roman soldier. The young Roman soldier was impressed at the quickness of Zadok's movement.

The Soldier smiled at Zadok to indicate that he meant no harm. His smile unknown to Zadok and just becoming apparent to the young Roman betrayed a growing affinity he had for the Children of Israel. This affinity would later be passed on to his children when he returned to his home in Germania. Within a generation or two his descendants would become some of the first European converts to the way of life followed by the Children of

Israel. In time his descendants would be viewed without distinction as the Children of Israel and deservedly so.

The officer of the young Roman soldier had no such affinity for the Children of Israel. He emerged from the darkness into the shadows and began to speak harsh words that Zadok did not understand. By now the servants assigned to accompany him, who had followed a respectable distance both in front and behind, hurried to the place where Zadok now stood. The young Roman soldier who now had Zadok's staff in his hand had begun to lower that staff to Zadok's side. Zadok offered no resistance but, was uncomfortable with his weapon; yes his weapon being touched by anyone other than him.

Two of the servants stepped into the shadows and began to chatter with the Roman officer as they fumbled for papers. After a brief period a servant motioned to Zadok to proceed. The other servants emerged from the shadows and gestured for him to do the same. Zadok looked at the young Roman soldier one last time. The soldier smiled again at Zadok as he turned away and stepped back into the shadows and the darkness.

The Temple

By now Zadok was wide awake and his body's cries for more rest had been put to rest. As they approached the Temple more Roman Soldiers came into view. The servants clustered around Zadok giving an indication to all that he was a person of some importance. However, it was rather strange for one so young to have so many guards. As guards it was so interpreted that the servants were assigned to protect young Zadok. If they only knew, Zadok was in the best position in a conflict to protect.

As young Zadok and his company arrived at the steps of the Temple all made way for this Son of what would have to be a very important Man. He looked for and saw the young man not much older than he. His name was Simon and he fit the description almost perfectly of the kind of Man Zadok was told by his grandfather to seek. This Simon greeted Zadok with a smile and Shalom. Zadok returned the greeting and other pleasantries as they both sat down and waited for the prayer. They would speak after the prayer.

Woodrow Manning Jr.

Lessons Learned From Grandfather Joshua
(Priests)

"Zadok?" "Yes, grandfather." "Pay attention, this is very important," said his grandfather Joshua. (This is how Zadok remembered the beginning of most lessons from his grandfather). "The priest is by profession a shepherd of the souls of his congregation. This charge obligates a priest to say and do what is best for each and every member. The priest with this charge is a target for any and all that would have him do what is best for them. Doing what is best for this special interest more often than not is bad for the congregation. A priest too comfortable with merchants and politicians is subjected to influences that causes him to overlook that which he should not. It causes him to say that which he should not and not say that which he should. It is believed that merchants and politicians have souls as well, (his grandfather would say half smiling) and are members of the congregation. They cannot be shunned or castigated simply because of their profession. However, socially they should be kept at arm's length. This is when the guard is down and if there is an opening. The merchants and politicians will take it."

Zadok remembers this lesson. He was 10 years old at the time.

Chapter 4

The Mission of Discovery

Zadok's Mission of Discovery was to make contact with the Messiah or his followers. There had been others sent before Zadok. Most were turned away from the City of David by the Romans. They returned to Fars without making any contact with the Messiah. These were the lucky ones. There were more than a few that never returned. They were never heard from again.

So it was a bit surprising when Zadok's Uncle David suggested that Zadok undertake this Mission of Discovery to the City of David. His grandfather did not like the idea but, after talking to Zadok's father, his grandfather offered no opposition to sending Zadok. Could it be that Zadok, his very own grandson, would lead and unite his people with the foretold "Messiah?" Joshua could only dream that it would be possible.

There at the Temple, not more than four days ago, following the directions of those that sent him, Zadok introduced himself to Simon and made a request. He wanted Simon to listen to his pronunciation of Hebrew from the sacred scrolls. Simon, at first suspicious, suggested that Zadok would be better served by asking one of the priests to listen. Zadok, quick with the answer, replied that he was more comfortable reciting with someone closer to his age. Someone possibly still yet a student? Seemingly reluctant, Simon agreed to listen.

Simon was young and not yet a priest. However, his attitude reflected his teachings. Zadok sensed that Simon was extremely scornful of some of the priests present at the Temple. His scorn was directed at those priests who dressed too well or in such a way that his grandfather would not approve. Such a well-dressed priest wore the clothing that pronounced prosperity and self-importance. The money for such clothing would have been better spent on the poor in grandfather's opinion. He was convinced that Simon felt this way also.

After the prayers Simon and Zadok would retire to a corner of the Temple under the watchful eye of many of the Elders present. If but not for the turbulent air throughout Palestine, they would have easily dismissed. The young man with this shepherd's staff made it necessary for many of the factions present to ask about who he may be. Those curious enough to investigate discovered that Zadok's father had business with Tobiad. This put them at ease. They had far greater concerns.

At the end of the seventh day of this routine, Zadok informed Simon that after the Sabbath he would be leaving for Fars. He continued that in all probability he would be returning with his father within the year. He hoped to see Simon the next time he visited the City of David. Simon replied that he too would be leaving the City of David and making a long journey. Zadok replied that if Simon would ever find himself in Fars Province, he and his family would be very easy to find. They parted company, neither knowing that they would see each other far sooner than expected.

Lessons Learned from Grandfather Joshua (Merchants)

Grandfather said, "Zadok, pay attention! What I am about to say is very important. Farmers are of all people in the very best of positions. They live off of the land. We are a family of farmers and we live off of the land. Everything that we need to sustain ourselves and our families we grow. The Sender of Messengers provides us with rain for the things that we plant. We store for the poor and hard times that which is in excess of our needs.

"Our business is as sheepherders. Yes, from time to time we do eat and sacrifice the sheep. We use the wool of the sheep to make the clothes that we wear. That which is in excess of what we need for food and clothing from the sheep we sell. We sell to those that make the carpets and tapestries in the cities.

"It is the merchant that buys these carpets and tapestries and sell them to others. The merchant does not live off of the land. The merchant lives off of differences. It is in the interest of the merchant to buy the carpet for less and to sell it for more."

"Are you paying attention Zadok," questioned his grandfather. "Yes grandfather." Zadok's grandfather continued, "It is the goal of the merchant to do everything that he can to buy for less and to sell for more. He does anything that he can to achieve this goal. Because of this, the priest must be very cautious when dealing with a merchant. If the merchant can manipulate the priest in any way to influence the congregation to buy more of that which the merchant sells, he will do it. As a priest you must, for the sake of your congregation, be careful about what you accept from merchants and say about them.

Zadok remembers this lesson. He was 14 years old.

The Merchant And The Banker

In the ten days that young Zadok visited the City of David with his father. They accomplished much more than they had hoped for. Zadok, not often given to self-praise, felt fairly pleased with himself. This trip also represented the first time that Zadok had spent with his father separate from his siblings. This gave him a chance to see that in more than physical appearance, Zadok was very much like his father. This pleased him a great deal. Zadok spent the next day and a half with his father. He abandoned his morning treks to the Temple of his Disappointment. Zadok reasoned this Temple was not the Temple of Solomon. There was no need for him to keep his pledge to pray there every morning. He had also learned from Simon that the High Priest was considering allowing the Roman to make sacrifices at the Temple. Sacrifices to the Roman pagan gods! Without a doubt, this place was not the Temple of Solomon! But still was it not the focal point of worship for his people? So in the company of his father he was to remain until their return trip to Fars.

Zadok watched with amazement as his father negotiated the final details of the business arrangements. Most of this time was spent with Tobiad and Eber. Eber was the son of his Great Uncle Caleb. He seemed to be a capable enough person as far as Zadok could tell. However, there was something that was not quite right about his character, or at least as Zadok perceived. Uncle Caleb arranged for the banker Tobiad to finance, on Eber's behalf, the trade deal with Zadok's father.

Zadok did not understand the ins and outs of the carpet and tapestry business. He did understand without anyone having to tell him that Eber was getting the table scraps. Aaron as much as he tried to mask his excitement, was getting far more than he expected. Zadok could feel his father's elation about the price they accepted. It was a rather surprising thing at that it was as if they were connected as with a string between them. He knew or felt what his father was doing. It was not about the money; although more money is always good - maybe? If put to good use his grandfather would add. For his father it was about the achievement. In time Zadok would completely understand.

As for the other side of the transaction, the banker clearly got the lion's share of the profit's plus. The banker got most of the distribution and sales profit. In addition Eber was paying the banker a fee for the cost of his money. Making a profit from the use of his money? Zadok did not understand that at all. As for the reason why Tobiad was doing the transactions at all, his motives were unclear. Zadok felt he took the money just because he could. Zadok did not like Tobiad if for no other reason than for the way he treated Eber.

Poor Cousin Eber mostly just sat silently as Tobiad and his father negotiated. Grandfather would tell Zadok, "Do not concern yourself with that which does not concern you." Clearly why cousin Eber would accept such conditions were of no concern to Zadok. But still, Eber was doing all of the work and getting, relatively speaking, so little money? Zadok understood now why at the dinner meeting ten days before, Cousin Eber sounded so sheepish. In retrospect it was a wonder he could find a voice to say anything at all. Zadok's thoughts kept coming back to the banker Tobiad. Why was he doing this transaction at all? Perhaps he would never know.

Lessons Learned From Grandfather Joshua (Bankers)

"Zadok pay attention! What I am about to say is very important," said Grandfather Joshua. "I must tell you about bankers. Bankers are people that have so much money they can loan their money to other people. This can be a very good thing. More often than not it is a very bad thing. It is bad for the people who borrow. People should try very hard to live within their means. It is bad for bankers because they can exploit people that need to borrow. Our family lives off of the land so we need very little money. Through our businesses in the city, we have been fortunate to make a lot of money. We make far more money than we need. We give a lot of this money away to help people. We don't give all of it away because we may need some of it in the future. We also help other businesses with our money and share in their profits. All the ways that our people can and cannot use money are in our laws. It is important for the priest to remember these ways and remind the people of these ways so that they do not stray".

Zadok remembers this lesson. He was 15 years old.

Departure From The City Of David

For both Zadok and Aaron the trip could be considered a very successful one. It would greatly add to the fortunes of the family of Nahor in the House of Joseph as his family was called. It would also add to the considerable prestige Aaron already had among the Persians, his grandfather so detested. His father already mastered the Greek and Persian that they spoke in Fars. Zadok noticed that in the time he had spent with Simon, his father had also picked up a rudimentary understanding of the language of the Romans.

Zadok prepared for the afternoon rest. The Caravan would depart for Fars later that evening. As the Axum people would say so said his grandfather, "If you want to go someplace fast go alone. But if you want to go someplace far go with a group." The trip back to Fars would be a long journey. There would be much to do in Fars before the return to the City of David. The success of his father's negotiating meant that they would return to the City of David sooner than later. Yes, there would be much to do before seeing his friend Simon again.

As Zadok fell asleep he was overcome by an overwhelming sense of confusion, shouting, memories of

Woodrow Manning Jr.

things that have not yet happened, sadness, and most of all grief.

Chapter 5

HISTORY I

(THOUGHTS OF A.B. NAAS)

While Zadok is, well for now, let us say sleeping. And clearly if you are reading this you are not. I thought that this would be a good place to remind you that in the introduction I mentioned History. Actually, after re-reading the introduction to these Chronicles as you just did or will do. I stated, "My Chronicles (record of history) are a journey around the circle of time." We have traveled a bit together and from time to time you may recognize what some would call history. These Chronicles are in fact in part a version of history. Ah, and what is history? Must it be written in order for it to be history? More questions yes.

Earlier, I asked you a question. Let me point out that you were asked this question in another space. So, travel back in space and revisit your answer to the question. Is it possible for a false fact to be true? If history is a record of events and events are facts then could there be such a thing as a false fact that is true? Could there be such a thing as a false fact period? Given that if it is an event then it must be a fact then it must be true, right? (It may be necessary to read that again. Go ahead I will not tell anyone). Oh, by the way keep reading and pay close attention, it is about to get very interesting.

Chapter 6

Family

Grandmother

Zadok's grandmother was beloved by all that knew her. If you lived in the Province of Fars you knew her. To Zadok she always smells of food. Not even the great magicians of Babylon could make as many things right as she could. The confusion, shouting, memories of things that have not yet happened, sadness, and grief, all began to dissipate as she spoke. Zadok focused on her voice unclear at first never the less firm and in command yet loving and soft. "Let him speak," she said. "It would be good for him to speak to us before..." It seems as if everyone present but, Zadok understood what these words meant. The shouting melted away as butter would on a hot surface. As for the people shouting, who were those people anyway? A bird called in the distance with a sound he had never heard before.

Zadok's clarity of thought came back to him as he began to remember his trip to Fars with his father. He had enjoyed the trip to the City of David with his father in spite of his disappointments. "Come, Zadok, and sit," his grandmother said. Zadok was still a bit dazed, not understanding why, but did just as he was told. "Come, I will get you something to eat," said his grandmother. Yes, the magic words: "something to eat!" Oh, how he had missed his grandmother's cooking. Most of all he missed the love and comforts that he was bathed in now in his grandfather's house. "Come, tell your grandfather all about your trip," she said. With that statement the confusion and all that accompanied it were reduced to the sounds of that distant bird calling unanswered to another.

Grandfather Joshua and three of his uncles that were also priests sat where they would normally sit in a family meeting of importance. Were they the ones doing the shouting? What were they shouting about and he thought he had heard women's voices? He clearly heard his mother's voice. Where was she? Before, Zadok could return to the confusion, "Zadok, tell us about your trip," his grandfather said. Zadok began to focus and laid out his report in just the way he had planned on the journey back to Fars from the City of David.

Zadok began to speak first of the City of David. As he began to speak it did not seem odd to him that he was not really speaking. It was as if he had been transported back to The City of David with grandfather and his uncles. There was no need for Zadok to explain that the air was foul, thick with the smell of garbage, sewage, the poor and the Romans. To Zadok and all that accompanied him there were just two categories of people: the clean or People of the Light; and the unclean, the People of Darkness.

Zadok explained in this new manner of communicating the tapestry of people present for prayer at the Temple. No need to explain why he did not refer to it as the Temple of Solomon. They clearly understood. The priests as well as all others present at the Temple were united by their common blood. Yes united in a way but, so divided in their attitude towards each other and the Romans.

As Zadok explained without explaining as his thoughts, he drifted to his grandfather. At the time this was not at all odd to Zadok. How could he explain so much without saying, well nothing? Zadok's grandfather was a proud son of the House of Joseph; son of Israel; son of Isaac; son of father Abraham. Zadok was taught from a very early age that he was part of the most noble bloodline. Joseph was Messenger, son of a Messenger, son of a Messenger, son of "The Messenger" father Abraham. "Zadok you have the noble blood of Messengers coursing through your veins!" his grandfather would say so proudly. "Never forget that!" his grandfather would conclude. Like all of the lessons from his grandfather, this lesson was etched permanently into Zadok's nature and character.

Father

Zadok was caught up in a whirlwind of confusion again. People were shouting; he could again hear his mother's voice. He was explaining to his grandfather and uncles the incident with the Roman soldiers. How could there be so much noise on this street in the City of David? There was no one else present so early that day except those Romans in the shadows and darkness. There was also that bird closer but, there was grandmother urging him to continue and he did. Like before but this time his thoughts were of his father.

Zadok's father Aaron did not have the intellect of his son. Nor did he have the intellect of his older brother David or any of his other brothers or sisters. This Zadok pieced together from comments made about his father by his brothers. (Zadok, as a child as some children do, would remain close enough to adults to hear what they were talking about. But far enough away so that they thought he could not hear them). Grandfather Joshua realized that Aaron was slow very early on. So he sent his father to work with grandfather's brother Shem in the city. This was according to his uncles. Clearly Aaron was not cut out to be a priest. But in the marketplace; he took to it like a duck takes to water.

Shem had done well in managing the family business. The business started by Zadok's Great-grandfather Nahor and his grandfather Joshua, traded fine hand woven Persian carpets and tapestries. (Would there ever be any other kind?) The business did very well under the stewardship of Shem. However, once Aaron entered the business the family within a generation became the wealthiest among all of the members of the House of Joseph in Fars Province.

Zadok's father could read people like the pages of a scroll. This ability gave him a distinct advantage in negotiating. He always bought lower than anyone and sold higher than everyone. Aaron negotiated a consolidation of most of the small producers in and around the Province of Fars. His trip to the City of David was an exploration into the possibilities of shipping these fine carpets to other territories within the Roman Empire. Maybe even Rome itself? He was invited to come to the city of David by his first cousin Eber, son of Caleb.

Woodrow Manning Jr.

Aaron loved Zadok as he did all of his six children. To say that Zadok was special would be true. Aaron had the ability to make everyone feel special. Perhaps he inherited this ability from his mother, Zadok's Grandmother. "Yes grandmother," Zadok answered. As Zadok turned away from his grandfather and uncles while explaining the caravan trip back to Fars. He turned to his grandfather and grandmother standing together holding hands. He had never seen them do that before. The call of that bird was closer - much closer. It was now too close to ignore. The shouting he could now understand, "Give them some space!" "He needs to have space! Give them some air! Get him some water!" he heard his mother say.

As those surrounding Zadok, his father came into focus and the confusion began to leave him. Zadok caught a glimpse of his grandfather and grandmother walking into the distance. He did not have words to explain or understand what he saw. The bird's calling was now so loud that he could not hear anything else. The realization that both his grandfather and grandmother had died while he was away slowly became his reality. As it did the bird calls began to lessen and then there was just silence and grief.

Fars

In the time it took Zadok to experience the meeting with his grandparents and uncles he had fallen from his horse. Zadok would later ponder how so much seemed to happen in such a short period of time. Both Zadok and his father collapsed upon hearing the news of the death of his grandmother and grandfather while they were away. In so doing, yet in another way, Zadok was like his father. At this time neither Zadok nor his father was conscience of this fact.

Zadok walked around in the haze of sadness at his parent's home in the city for a number of days. Zadok could not bear going back to the village that he had called home from his earliest memory that would now be absent his grandparents. He knew that his Uncle David would be expecting him in that now Uncle David was the head of the family of Joshua. The report that he had so meticulously laid out in his mind for his grandfather on the caravan trip home would now have to be delivered to Uncle David. Zadok had to proceed to the village. It was the noble thing to do.

After the Sabbath, Zadok rode to the village alone. Upon arriving at the village there were many tears. He greeted his uncles and aunts and many cousins as a

"Comforter" of sorts. Somehow this made him feel better by not focusing on his own grief. Instead his focus was on the grief of all those who now came to him. Zadok drew strength from the memory of his grandparents holding hands. The image of them walking into that which he did not have the words to describe, explain, or understand gave him a sense of Shalom.

After the evening meal at what used to be his grandparents' home, Zadok along with his uncles went into the meeting room. With his grandfather absent, Zadok presented his report to his Uncle David who now sat in the Seat of Authority.

The Mission

The Mission had actually been the brainchild of Zadok's Uncle David, or so it seemed at time. In a way it was fitting that Zadok presented his report to Uncle David. Uncle David had the pleasant easy going manner of Zadok's grandmother - most of the time. It was believed by many that his intellect surpassed that of the considerable one possessed by Zadok's grandfather. No one knew for sure in that Uncle David would only speak in the presence of his father when asked to do so by his father. He loved and respected his father above all others. Well, almost all others. There was his mother, of course. He treated her as if the very gates of Paradise lie at her feet.

Zadok spoke of his rationale for choosing Simon. Uncle David and the two of his uncles present expressed approval of his choice. Simon, as per their collective instructions, was the perfect choice as the object of his mission. Simply put, the Mission was to make contact with someone in the Movement began by the "Messiah." Talk of another "Messiah" had reached Fars before. This new one - this Joshua - was different. The things that he could do, if proven true, would represent clear evidence; that he was the promised "Messiah" that Zadok's people were waiting for. Zadok was advised not to move too quickly in the City of David. To do so would have drawn attention of the type that would have complicated future plans. His people had been patience for more than a few hundred years waiting for the "Messiah" to appear. To wait a little longer, be it a year or two or even a few hundred years more, was a duty they owed to both the "Messiah" and the "Comforter."

During Zadok's entire presentation he never expressed that in his personal opinion he considered this Joshua the so called "Messiah." Those present were not

Woodrow Manning Jr.

interested in his personal opinion. In time that, and many other things concerning Zadok, would change.

Chapter 7

The Village Of Joshua

As Zadok finished his presentation and discussion with his uncles it occurred to him that the placed that he had called home was now the home of his Uncle David. He began to fidget a bit before asking where he could sleep for the night. His Uncle David looked at him with some surprise and asked, "What is wrong with your room? Is it not just as you left it?" Zadok started to speak but could not voice the words as he began to cry. All of the brothers embraced Zadok and each other as they all cried there together silently. Their shared grief was in missing their grandparents and father.

The next day Zadok visited the cave were the bodies of his grandparents were decaying. It was the custom of his people to dress the bodies of the deceased in the burial shawl and seal the bodies in a cave for a year. They would then return to the cave and collect the bones and store them. It was the hope of his people that their bones would one day be buried in the City of David.

Zadok's cousin Maryum had walked with him to the burial cave. They had always been very close. She was very happy to be of help to him at this extremely difficult moment. No one had explained before that grandmother died first. It was believed that grandfather was so grief stricken that he died in his sleep the day after. To lose one of the pillars of the family was hard enough; but to lose both. They were both silent as they held hands on the walk back to the village. From that day forward Zadok would call the village the Village of Joshua.

In the distance Zadok saw the profile of his Uncle David as they returned. As they approached him Maryum continued walking after greeting her father. Zadok stopped just before reaching him. Uncle David invited Zadok to walk with him to the public drinking well. On the way, he began to speak. To Zadok's shock and surprise Uncle David indicated the he wanted Zadok to go work for his father Aaron in the city.

Uncle David went on to explain that a war was coming between the forces of darkness and the forces of light. Without saying it, Uncle David expressed that he felt that the forces of light were ill equipped to engage in such a battle. Their natural allies were all weakened to the point of being helpless. The Might People of Axum were but a shadow of their former might and glory. The Aramaic speaking tribes were so busy fighting among themselves that they could see no further than their next conflict. The poor sons of Ishmael - all they had to offer was sand and rocks or so Uncle David thought.

All that was left was the House of Joseph there in Fars.

Lessons Learned From Grandfather Joshua (The House of Joseph)

"Zadok are you paying attention?" "Yes grandfather," said Zadok. "Joseph was the noblest man to have ever lived. He was a Messenger; he was the son of a Messenger, he was the Grandson of a Messenger, and the Great Grandson of the Great Messenger Abraham. A great betrayal had been done by his brothers to Joseph. While he acknowledged this betrayal, he forgave them. His descendants too acknowledged the betrayal and they two would not forget what had been done. But, they moved on.

"When Joshua and Caleb led the Children of Israel into the land they would call home they divided the land according to tribes. The House of Joseph was given some of the most fertile land with an abundance of water. This did not set too well with some of the other tribes. Over the years the resentment of the House of Joseph grew into hatred. Of all the tribes, the House of Judah received the most land. Some say this was done because they were the largest tribe. Others would say this was done in hopes of satisfying their greed. Not all of the members of the Children of Israel felt hatred towards the House of Joseph. Most of the members of the Children of Israel did not feel anything but love and affection for the House of Joseph and each other. However, members of the House of Judah ignored the will and the affection of the people. They sent a delegation to the Assyrians with an offer. The offer was that the other Tribes of the Children of Israel would offer no resistance if the Assyrians would invade the land of the House of Joseph. Furthermore, they could take away the members of the house of Joseph with all of their wealth and possessions.

"This offer was too good to be refused. The Assyrians invaded the land of the House of Joseph and took them away in bondage. Not one of the other Tribes of the Children of Israel lifted a finger to help the House of Joseph. Not even the Tribe of Benjamin. All actions have their associated consequences. When good people set back and let bad things happen to other good people. Can they not expect the same for themselves some day?

"A few years later Nebuchadnezzar the King of Babylon thought it was a good idea to invade the land of the Children of Israel. He dragged "all" of them off into captivity in the same way that the House of Joseph had been taken. Nebuchadnezzar did not stop with this act. He destroyed the Temple of Solomon and took all of its treasures back to Babylon.

"Mercy being what it is, Cyrus the Great freed the Children of Israel from their captivity by the Babylonians. In addition, he also freed the House of Joseph from their captivity by the Assyrians. The Children of Israel went back to their homes in Palestine. Many in the House of Joseph wanted nothing more to do with the Tribe of Israel or as they were becoming the Tribe of Judah. So, the House of Joseph settled in Persia along the silk route. They made their living as farmers, sheep herders, and general traders. They vowed never to return to the City of David until the coming of the Messiah.

"They also made a separate and secret vow to never be taken captive again. To this end they developed as many of their men as were capable into master warriors. Capable of subduing or killing 10 men equally armed and equipped. There standard weapon was the Shepherd's staff. With a twist of the wood in the right place it became a pike capable of stopping any charging man or animal. With the press of a button and a pull and twist of the staff it became a sword made of bronze. This sword, while light, would break any iron sword like a piece of glass smashed against a solid brick wall."

"Zadok this is your staff. You will begin your lessons today. You are beginning the process of become a man. The mastery of this staff is a part of that process. Let us begin," so said Joshua to Zadok's grandfather.

Rachel

Zadok's wife and daughter lived in his in-laws' village. The next day Zadok got up early to make the half day's ride to be with them. Marriage, when it is right, is bliss on earth. More often than not, this takes time. When it is wrong; well let's just say it is something else. Zadok's marriage to Rachel was an arranged marriage designed to bring two families closer together. The marriage in fact did just that - the families were closer. Zadok felt as if he was the sacrificial lamb used to bring about this union. He often envisioned himself on a table with an apple in his mouth, cooked and ready for each of the families to take a slice of him that would do them the most good.

Rachel was pleasant enough. It's just that to Zadok she looked more like the trunk of a big tree than a woman he should desire. Her face was not pretty nor was she unattractive. She had two eyes, a nose and a mouth. She had ears also, so all of the parts where there. Her shoulders were broader than his and could carry more weight. Once while Zadok was helping her father off load linen from a wagon, Rachel pitched in to help. Zadok's knees buckled under the weight of one bundle. Rachel threw one bundle over one shoulder and another over the opposite shoulder. Zadok feared the she would offer to carry him and the bundle he was struggling with as well.

All is not displeasing to Zadok about Rachel. She has given him the joy of his life - his daughter Ambra. He was not sure where the name came from. It had been handed down by the women of Rachel's family for generations. And neither did he care. To see his daughter smile was as if one saw the sun rise for the first time. Her laugh was infectious and no matter what he was doing he had to stop. Just so that he could enjoy the laugh and fully appreciate the warmth it brought to his heart. Ambra was the love of his life and his reason for wanting a better world.

The Great Escapes

In between the time Zadok was being drained by Rachel, as he viewed it, and the time he spent hiding from her. He often sought refuge behind the bolts of linen stored by Rachel's father. The warehouse, if it could be called that, had many places to hide. Rachel saw it as a game of finding Zadok. Zadok saw it as no game, instead he thought of it as surviving Rachel.

Zadok's time in hiding gave him time to think. He thought back to the dinner he attended with his father at the rich merchant's home in the City of David. He considered all of the things that were being said about the so-called "Messiah." If he could really do all of the things that were said about him, he had to be the "Messiah" and the long awaited Messenger. He also reconsidered the advice he was given to not be too aggressive in his inquiries about the Messiah. Maybe he should have asked Simon more questions he thought?

While he did not question Uncle David at the time, he now wondered why now he was being asked to go to the city and work with his father. Having time away from Rachel was more than a sufficient reason to be anywhere but where she was. This last thought made him feel guilty. Was she not a good mother to his beloved Ambra?

Was she not a good cook who by all evidence loved her food as much if not more than anyone? Most of all he did miss her while he was away. Yes, he was feeling a bit guilty hiding behind the looms of fabric. Then he heard her call in that shrill but playful voice, "Zadok where are you?" At that point all guilt disappeared; the only thing that he could think of now was where else he could hide!

Ruben

Rachel's father Ruben was a dealer in dyes and fabrics. He often made trips to Babylon to visit the Magicians. These Magicians provided Ruben with the mixtures he used as dyes for his fabrics. Mixtures from the Magicians of Babylon can be used for many things. It had been rumored that he had another family there in Babylon but this was said only in whispers.

During the evenings after Rachel had finished with Zadok, they took the short walk to visit her parents after dinner. On one such visit, Rachel's father announced that he would be visiting Babylon in a few days. Without hesitating Zadok offered to join his on his trip. All were surprised in that Zadok had shown no interest in his father-in-law's business. Zadok, sensing this, explained that he would now be working with his father in the city.

Woodrow Manning Jr.

The more he knew about dyes, the greater the possibility he could find increased uses of his father-in-law's products. Rachel viewed his comments with a suspicion look.

Zadok's father-in-law was delighted by this news. His son-in-law would now be working directly with the richest merchant in all of Fars. This could only mean more business and markets for his products. Rachel was far less than excited. Zadok's father-in-law announced that they would leave in the morning. Zadok knew it was going to be a long night as he looked at Rachel and she smiled.

Chapter 8

The Trip To Babylon

The next morning Zadok and his father-in-law set out for Babylon. They would only be gone a few weeks. Traveling was made all the more difficult for Zadok by the soreness in his loins put there by Rachel. He welcomed the trip just to give his body a rest. That was until he realized that his father-in-law was droning endlessly. He wanted Zadok to know that he could do a lot more business if he had more capital. Without saying it directly, he wanted Zadok to approach his father to invest in his business.

Zadok was beginning to wonder which was worst. He thought Rachel's insatiable desires and imagination that at times had him feeling like a twisted piece of pastry. But maybe his father-in-law's droning endlessly of his need for more capital for his business was worse. After two days into their seven day journey to Babylon, Zadok suggested that maybe he should suggest to his father that investing in Ruben's business would be a good idea. His father-in-law beamed with a smile as bright as the full moon on a dark night. The rest of the trip was peaceful for Zadok. This peace gave him time to think.

So much had happened during his trip to the City of David, his return to Fars, and now his uncle wanted him to go work for his father. This last one caused him the most concern and puzzlement. Clearly, his grandfather wanted him to be a priest. His grandfather even expressed hope that maybe even Zadok would be the head priest in all of Fars. His Uncle David had changed the direction of Zadok's life. Not that he minded in that he, like all of the members of his family, and most of the House of Joseph lived to serve. This oath was taken upon entering manhood, but still?

Babylon

Zadok had never been to Babylon before. It, like the City of David, was just a shadow of its former self. But still there resided in the city, magicians of extraordinary knowledge and power. Zadok was particularly interested in speaking to those magicians or anyone, who could shed light on how the so-called "Messiah" performed his miracles. His father-in-law sent him to those magicians that he was most familiar. He found no one to help explain until he was sent to Harut.

Harut seemed as old as time itself. Zadok presented his questions about the so-called "Messiah" to Harut. Then he asked, "was it magic?" Harut gave Zadok the following understanding, "Magic is deception. A slight of the hand a trick played on one's vision." The things that Zadok spoke of regarding the ability of the "Messiah" Joshua, represented real power emanating from the source of all power.

Harut gave Zadok the story of Moses and his encounter with the Magicians of Pharaoh. The Magicians of Pharaoh seeking favor from Pharaoh sought to outdo the magic of Moses. When they discovered that Moses was using no magic and the power he had exposed their magic as false, they bowed down and proclaimed that they believed in the Lord of Moses and Aaron. All who encounter the power spoken of by Zadok would do themselves a favor, if they were to do the same as the magicians of Pharaoh, Harut added.

Zadok now had more information and understanding than he had hoped for. He offered to pay Harut to which Harut declined. Harut concluded with, "my reward is from my Lord. What you offer me is of no value." Zadok said, "May That which knows all be with you." Harut smiled and the smile was understood.

For the next couple of days Zadok took in the sights of Babylon. One of the most amazing things he saw was a light with no flame. The magician placed two wires in a fluid and it caused the light to glow within the glass. There were all kinds of magicians with potions promising to cure everything from baldness to consumption. There was one magician who sold nothing but aids for marriage relationships. Zadok spent a fair amount of money with this magician.

In addition, he really enjoyed the Puppet Shows. Watching the Puppet Masters pull the strings of the different characters as he put words in their mouths. He had never seen anything like that before in Fars. (Or so he thought).

Zadok saw very little of his father-in-law for the entire week that they were in Babylon. This would lend further speculation that he had other business there that had nothing to do with dyes. To Zadok it was of little to no concern in that while he would listen to gossip, he would not spread gossip. After twelve days in Babylon, the two of them departed for Fars Province.

Men May Plan

When Zadok and Ruben reached the village they called home, Zadok's wife came out to greet them with a very worried look on her face. This caused Zadok's heart to sink and he became a bit light headed. The memory of the shock of losing his grandparents was still a very raw nerve. She indicated that his father left word for him to come to the city as soon as he returned from Babylon. And so without hesitation he set out for Shiraz.

After the half day's ride to the Village of Joshua, Zadok and his horse were exhausted. He made the executive decision to stay overnight at what was now his Uncle's David home. To his surprise he found his Uncle David waiting for him. Though tired to the point of near collapse, he shared a meal with his Uncle and then adjourned to the meeting room. There David informed Zadok that four visitors from the City of David had come to Shiraz looking for him. His Uncle David speculated that the reason for the visit had something to do with the "Messiah." Zadok could not add any more to his uncle's guess about the nature of the visit or the visitors.

Instead of feeling a need to say something more, Uncle David laid out his plan for the future direction of the family. He explained to Zadok that it was his belief that the world was about to enter into a long period of darkness. In this darkness the truth would be considered the lie and the lie will be considered the truth. It was necessary for those who serve the truth and justice to fight against this coming darkness, but in the end they will lose. Uncle David paused for a considerable amount of time to let his words sink in.

He continued by saying that the time and approach of Zadok's grandfather was over, and would serve no purpose against the encroaching darkness. Priests cloistered, isolated, and removed from the world will not help the people. That is why he wanted Zadok to go work for his father and learn the business. Zadok's generation and the ones to follow would have to straddle two worlds. They would have to live in the material world and also master coexistence with their spirituality. In other words, find a way to say what should be said to the politicians, business men, and to the people in general.

Uncle David reminded Zadok of his grandfather's opinion regarding priests who were too comfortable with business people and politicians. Uncle David expressed agreement with his father's assessment. However, in this new world of darkness the priest, out of necessity, will have to deal with both the business people and the politicians in all circles. He went on to say that there will be a struggle. Most priests will lose and become pawns to the business people and politicians. The people will suffer greatly because of the co-opting of the priests. This will prolong the darkness.

Zadok was now at the point of wanting to get back on his horse and ride as fast and as long as he could away from all of this. He had rarely felt so depressed and hopeless. After an indeterminate amount of time he asked his uncle was there any hope at all. His uncle replied, "Of course there is." Uncle David went on to say that the hope rested in the message of the Messiah. He had sent word to Zadok's father to bring the guest to the village, in so doing this would save Zadok a trip to the city. Not to mention by having the meeting in the village, David would now be present and find out directly why they had come so far to see Zadok.

Zadok was a bit puzzled in that how did Uncle David know that they had a message from the "Messiah." Uncle David responded that just as they were looking for the Messiah. The "Messiah" would have been looking for them. Zadok, a young man with a shepherd's staff in the City of David, was a sign for those who could see and understand it. It was amazing to Zadok that Uncle David had figured all of this out before he sent him to the City of David. He never considered the possibility that maybe;

just maybe, Uncle David was trying to make an impression.

Zadok had one last question before he dragged himself off to get some rest. "Uncle David," he asked, "what if they have no message from the Messiah?" Without hesitating Uncle David said, "Then the last breath that they take will be in this village." With that Zadok went off to bed. As usual his last thoughts were of Rachel and the warmth and softness of her body.

Chapter 9

The Unseen Realities

(Thoughts Of A.B. Naas)

It has been said by those who study such things that 97% of all the matter in the Universe is unseen. If you can't see it, then how do they know it is there? They know that it is there because of the effect that it has on all of the things that we can see.

In telling a story such as the one you are reading, it would be safe to assume that there are parts that impact greatly on the story that are not being told. For example, why did Zadok's cousin Maryum walk with him to the cave where their grandparents' bodies were decaying? That is a great story worth telling but - not here and not now.

Chapter 10

The Visitors From The City Of David

Before the midday meal and rest the servants spotted seven riders approaching the village from the city. It was assumed that four of the riders were the "visitors." One would be Zadok's father and it was anyone's guess about the others. A roasted calf was prepared to welcome the visitors. The meeting would take place at the community meeting area in back of the Temple. Zadok began to wonder if that place was chosen if they did not have news about the "Messiah." Well, what would be done next would best be done out of sight.

As they arrived in the village, Zadok recognized his friend Simon from the Temple. They were pleased to see each other. The man leading the group was called James. A slight man with an easy going serene persona and curiously he carried a shepherd's staff. He was accompanied by a man named Peter and another named

Barnabas. The other two men were priests from the city. One of which Zadok never expect to see again.

The two priests that he recognized were Abraham from the House of Joseph and Enoch from the Tribe of Levi. Abraham was a contemporary of his Uncle David and also a student of his grandfather. Abraham had moved to the city and became a priest at one of smaller Temples (there were five in Shiraz). The other priest Enoch; Zadok had only seen once. That was about ten years ago. Enoch's presence there in the Village of Joshua was a sad reminder to Zadok that grandfather was now gone.

They all exchanged pleasantries and were invited to sit and enjoy a meal together. James, Simon, Peter nor Barnabas would eat any meat. However, they seemed to enjoy all of the other food that was prepared. Uncle David suggested that they rest until the noontime heat dissipated. They would speak in detail later after the evening meal. The guests were shown to one guest house and the others headed to a second guest house.

Second Guest House

At the second guest house, they each shared what they had learned from the visitors. The priest Abraham was a distant cousin of Zadok's family. He indicated that James was the leader of the group. He went on to say that, James was the most insightful person about revelation he had ever met. Each and every question put to James was answered. He answered in such a way that added knowledge with insight Abraham never considered. In addition he appeared to have knowledge of Revelations that he had not heard before. He knew it was Revelation because it flowed seamlessly with all that they knew as Revelation. "Well that's taking it a bit too far" Enoch was quick to say. "No man could make those words fit together that well! No matter how brilliant he may be," replied Abraham undeterred.

The others were loyal companions of James. It seemed as if James and Simon may have been related in some way. Perhaps Simon was a younger brother to James? Barnabas was very close to both. Peter was in a class of his own. To say that he was like a rock would only begin to describe his presences. Peter was more like an unshakable mountain.

"What did they say of the 'Messiah,'" Uncle David asked. "Nothing! Not a thing. They wanted to make their presentation to the Council," said the priest Abraham. "Well, there is not going to be a Supreme-Council meeting until I know much more than this," Uncle David said in a huff. To the surprise of Uncle David, Aaron replied, "The arrangements have already been made. The Supreme-Council will convene this evening. The Council of Elders thought that the information that I presented to them a few days ago was sufficient to call a meeting." Zadok could not be certain but, he thought that his father got at least a small amount of satisfaction from Uncle David's reaction.

Zadok had no idea what a Supreme-Council Meeting entailed. What was even more interesting was that Uncle David appeared to be fuming. Zadok did not know why and would have pondered this question more. However, his father's posture communicated, to anyone who did not know, that he was in charge. Zadok's impression of his father was as if he was watching one of the Puppet Masters in Babylon. Clearly, he had outdone Uncle David. At what he did not know, but that changed nothing.

No other comments were made. With that they each went to take their afternoon rest.

The Short Walk

The heat of the day had broken and they had all taken their rest. Zadok was milling around and noticed Simon doing the same. He called over to him and asked if he could use some company. To which Simon replied, "of course" and Zadok walked over to join his friend. After saying how good it was to see each other again. Simon commented on the beauty of the countryside.

Zadok asked him a question that he had been thinking about for a while. "Why were you really at the Temple of Solomon that first day I approached you?" Not wanting to offend Simon he called it the Temple of Solomon even though he thought of it as otherwise. "Why do you ask," questioned Simon. "Well you just seemed to be there alone. You were not reacting with anyone just looking around," replied Zadok. "I was looking for you," Simon replied. "How could you have been looking for me when you did not know that I would be there," questioned Zadok. "Actually, he knew someone like you would eventually come," said Simon with a smile. Zadok thought for just a moment and then realized Simon said, "He knew." Zadok said, "You mean?!" All Simon would do was just smile. And the smile was understood.

Before Zadok could ask another question Simon stated that there had been others. Many other who came looking but, less than a handful had actually made it to the Temple. Some, they were able to intercept before they got to the city of David. Others, they suspect, the

Roman got to before they could. For the moment Zadok was distracted as he remembered the faces of those priests from Fars that were sent but never returned.

Simon got Zadok's attention when he said with a chuckle, "If you can believe it, the Roman's actually sent a few themselves but they were easy to spot." In anticipation of Zadok's next question of how? Simon explained, "The Covenant that we safeguard as a people is both the Word and the Traditions. As it was the tradition of Moses to carry such a shepherd's staff into the very court of the Pharaoh. Anyone looking for Him would have known and understood the Symbolism of the shepherd's staff. They would as you did have one. It is very difficult to deceive him."

"Him," Zadok said. "Yes, 'Him,' the 'Messiah,'" said Simon. "Have you met the 'Messiah?'" said Zadok, in a wide eyed question. Still more than just a bit weary from his trip from Babylon, then to the Village of Joshua, his attention was now completely focused as Simon said, "Of course." "What is he like? Is he still alive? Did you see him do all of the things they said he has done? Where is he now!?" Before Zadok could continue with his rapid fire questions Simon said, "I can say no more. All that you need to know about the 'Messiah' for now will be told by James later."

"Well, can you answer me this one question," asked Zadok. To which Simon replied, "If I can." "Is the Messiah still alive"? To which Simon replied without hesitating, "Yes. And very much so," he added with a wide smile. Zadok did not know why but, Simon's answer lifted the equivalent of a boulder off of his chest. Maybe it was because of the conversation he had with Uncle David the day before. If the Messiah is still alive there is hope that the battle against the forces of darkness could be won. He would later reflect back on this moment when he is much older. His thoughts at that time will be the power of just a word.

As they walked in silence a bit more, a servant came running to Zadok to let him know that his father needed to see him right away. Simon indicated that he wanted to enjoy the countryside a bit more and told Zadok to go and that he would be fine. With that, Zadok and the servant went to see his father.

Colors

Zadok walked back to his grandfather's house where his father and Uncle David were waiting for him. Their posture was a bit strange. It left Zadok with the feeling that he had as a child when he had done something and tried to hide it from his grandmother. As best as he could recall without exception his grandmother found it. His father and Uncle David asked Zadok to join them in the meeting room. This only added to his feeling that he had been caught. Caught doing what he did not know, but they had him and there was no escape.

Once in the meeting room things changed and he saw three shepherd's staffs standing upright in a rest. They each took a seat and his father began to speak. He told the story of the Messenger Joseph as a young boy and the envy that his older brothers had for him and his younger brother Benjamin. Part of the source of the envy was that Joseph's father had given him a very beautiful over garment of many colors. This over garment was befitting Joseph because of his character, good nature, and nobility.

The colors from that time to their present have been a symbol for the Sons of the House of Joseph of Merit. From one generation to the next the colors were earned. The colors, seven in all, are only displayed openly on very special occasions. The meeting that they were about to have, with the guest, was just such an occasion. Zadok has earned the privilege of a color. In addition he has earned a place in the Supreme Council.

Zadok would be attending such a meeting for the first time. It was explained that at just 16 years old, it was an honor for him that the Council of Elders has elevated him to the position of Guardian of the Covenant. Zadok had no idea what any of this meant. He knew that there were Elders but a Council of Elders? Zadok did not move a muscle.

As a Guardian of the Covenant he had to pledge to do anything and everything in his power to protect the Covenant given to the Sons of Isaac. In addition he had to pledge to carry out the assignment given to him to the upmost best of his ability. Zadok pledged to do both. He did not know it at the time but, he would be called upon many times to carry out his pledge. With that they handed him his new shepherd's staff. They wrapped Zadok in the colors and walked together to the Temple in the Village of Joshua.

Chapter 11

The Supreme Council

As they approached the Temple, Zadok noticed that there were guards standing at the door of the Temple and throughout the Temple grounds. This was in itself strange but it was even stranger because he did not recognize any of them. They all wore black, carried pikes, and had swords at their sides. As they approach the first guard they were asked firmly to, "Make known yourselves." His father and Uncle David unsheathed their shepherd's staffs and Zadok did the same. The guard responded by saying, "Welcome O Sons of Joseph. You may proceed."

Zadok had a passing thought which he quickly dismissed in that it was he that should be doing the welcoming. After all, that was his Temple built by his forefathers. And besides who were these strangers anyway? As they got to the Temple doors they were each greeted in the same way as the guard before. This time they were told separately to follow a different marshal. They were each taken in separate directions and for the first time Zadok noticed that his father's shepherd's staff had more colors than his Uncle David's staff.

The Temple meeting room had been completely rearranged. There were no chairs and the room itself was in a horseshoe formation with the center of the room completely free of either sitting pillows or chairs. Zadok was not sure how they did it but the room was arranged in tier. He was taken to the fourth tier and correctly assumed that this was the level for those who had the least amount of rank.

On either side of him were two men, neither of which he had ever seen or met before. They were pleasant enough and as Zadok looked around the room he saw less than 10 people that he recognized. There were well over 100 men of various ages in the room. Zadok slowly began to realize that he was now part of the Supreme Council of the Sons of Joseph. This was the ruling body above all others governing the affairs of his people. He still had not figured out what he had done to be given such an honor. For a moment he thought that he should tell someone that there must be some mistake. He did not belong there. He did the wise thing in doing nothing.

As he looked around the room he noticed that his father was on the first level and that his Uncle David was on the third level in a different section. One of the two elders from his village he recognized was also on the first level as his father, but in a different section. The other six people he recognized were either on his level or on the one below. Zadok thought to himself that it would take forever for him to figure out the meaning of the placement in seating. Without any notice a priest began reciting a prayer. The room became silent and afterward the meeting began.

The Clear Evidence

The priest Abraham from the city walked into the center of the room. He requested permission to address the elders present in a manner for all to hear. There were seven elders sitting at the center of the horseshoe formation. They all nodded that he could do so. He was understandably nervous. He steadied himself and made his presentation. With the exception of the seven elders, Zadok, his Uncle David, his father and Abraham the priest, no one present knew why they were all summoned to this gathering. Zadok considered, just for a moment, that putting together such a gathering must have taken a lot of effort. He had not learned yet that there were those present who had mastered the use of birds to communicate messages over large distances.

As Abraham got further into his presentation it began to dawn on those gathered why they were there. The priest Abraham was about to present proof that the "Messiah" has appeared. There had been rumors before of the appearance of the "Messiah," most of which were quickly dismissed. Never before have they been summoned to specifically discuss the issue of the "Messiah," in addition to consider proof. The gravity of this gathering caused many in the room to look to and fro to see if everyone understood what they themselves were hearing.

As Abraham concluded his presentation, he requested permission to bring representatives of the "Messiah" into the room. The Elders nodded and Abraham left the room to get the guests. At this point the room was all a buzzed. Could it be possible that in their lifetime the "Messiah" would appear? One of the Elders said, "Silence please!" and as he did James with his shepherd's staff, Peter, Barnabas and Simon entered the room. The room became so quiet that if the blinking of the eye made a sound, it would have been comparatively thunderous.

James walked into the center of the room ahead of the others and stopped just short of the Elders. He greeted them in the customary manner and turned to greet all present in the room. James introduced himself as James the son of Joseph. He began to speak without provocation but, he took complete control of the room and everyone in it. He spoke not loud nor soft but with authority and firmness. Zadok sensed a sort of sadness in his serenity.

Finally, he stated that he was sent by the "Messiah" with a New Covenant. The New Covenant confirmed and reaffirmed all that represented the essence of the Old Covenant. The New Covenant lifted some of the burden from the Children of Israel placed on them by the transgression of their forefathers. In addition, the New Covenant charged the Children of Israel with laying the foundation for the "Comforter."

If you were to ask how long he spoke it is doubtful if anyone could tell you. The entire room was transfixed on his every word. When he finished there was silence. One of the Elders broke the silence by asking the question, "Should we accept that what you say is true because you say it is so?" James replied, "No, here is my proof." With that he unsheathed the covered portion of his shepherd's staff. The entire staff glowed as brightly as the sun at mid-day. The Elders first, and then everyone else in the room prostrated themselves in the direction of prayer weeping uncontrollably. They were given "clear evidence."

Chapter 12

Light

(THOUGHTS OF A.B. NAAS)

There is a lot that can be said about light. There are branches of sciences devoted to just the study of light. Needless to say, there are people that know a lot more about light than I do. What I would like to do, and forgive me for saying this. I would like to shed some light on the frequent use of the word light throughout this book and the Chronicles.

Sight, all sight is based on light. It is not to be confused with perception. Perception may or may not require light. Light, or let us say white light, contains all of the colors. So when you look at something and it appears to be the color blue. In actuality blue is the only color that is not being absorbed by the object you are looking at. Blue is actually the color that is being rejected (reflected) by the object you are looking at and back to your eyes. Your eyes will then pass on that information to your brain and it recognizes the color blue. For the moment let's lay aside the physics of refraction and other dynamics that can affect your perception of colors.

The Messenger Joseph according to some traditions was given an over garment of many colors by his father. I mentioned this only because colors have a long tradition in the House of Joseph. In the House of Joseph, rank was measured by the number of colors that were earned. Please note colors were never given. All of the colors had to be earned.

So when James, son of Joseph, unsheathed his shepherd's staff and it glowed as bright as the mid-day sun (with no heat). The Elders first recognized that the holder of the staff out ranked everyone in the room. There was no need to mention which Tribe or House he belonged. The white light containing all colors said all that needed to be said. James, the son of Joseph, and his relationship with the Messiah was not the issue. The "clear evidence" was for their acceptance of the Messiah. It was meant specifically just for them. (What an Honor and tremendous responsibility!).

This was a sign clearly meant for them and without any ambiguity they understood. All they could do was submit. Easier for some than for others, but we will get to that... (Of course given time and space).

Chapter 13

After And Before

It has been six weeks since the "Event." That is what Zadok called what occurred at the Supreme Council Meeting. It was forbidden by punishment that could be as severe as death, to discuss anything that was said or occurred at any Supreme Council Meeting. This rule was just one of the many rules given to Zadok regarding the conduct of Supreme Council Members. "Junior Supreme Council Member" is how he was addressed and welcomed by the others. Unbeknownst to him he was nominated by his grandfather to become a member of the Supreme Council should he be successful on his mission.

It was clear to all judging, that the mission was successful even before the proof or "clear evidence" was presented. Zadok had gotten closer than any of his predecessors on discovering the truth about the "Messiah" Joshua. There were many tests and challenges leading up to Zadok's nomination as a Council member. Unknown to Zadok he was always being watched. Others had plans for him that if he had known of them, he would have run as far and as fast as he could to get away. But then again, is this not the same true of each person's unknown future?

The City

Zadok, to the consternation of his cousins and uncles there in the city, was now working with his father. Their lack of warmth and brisk nature did not bother him. As a matter of fact he hardly noticed. What he did notice was that many of the strange faces he saw at the Temple. He now saw them at the business and they worked directly for his father. They were part of the crew his father used to guard the caravans that carried their carpets. Equally, or at least just as important they made sure that the money got back to Fars. Among them were members of the House of Joseph, the Sons of Ismail, and the Axum People. A strange but then again not so strange mixture for what they were trained and equipped to do.

While at work Zadok would often be found just staring into space completely unaware of what was happening around him. The light emanating from the staff held by James, son of Joseph, was all he could think about. To look into it and see every color imaginable mesmerized him every time he thought about it. He thought about it often.

He also remembers his interaction with Harut in Babylon. Was that his name Harut? Or was it Marut? One or the other he believed it was. So much was communicated to Zadok that day. Zadok was convinced that the light held by James, son of Joseph, was no magic. It was real power emanating from the source of all power. It had to be true he thought, right?

Zadok did not care much for city life. His father had him working on various projects with his cousins involving people who were speaking anything but Hebrew. Zadok was completely clueless at first but slowly he was beginning to pick up words and phrases. His cousins were not at all helpful. They seemed to go out of their way to speak faster or use colloquial speech to further confuse Zadok. Zadok did not seem to mind; he had other things to ponder. Rachel was pregnant with their second child.

In addition to everything else that was different; his father introduced him to this strange character; a son of Ishmael by the name of Ahmed. Zadok enjoyed his company and it gave him the chance to speak the language of the Children of Ishmael. Ahmed was very precise in his pronunciation of words in his native tongue. He insisted that Zadok also be precise when speaking to him in his language. With fairly a bit of amusement to Zadok, Ahmed spent the better part of a day teaching him the difference between the pronunciation of Ta and Tah. Zadok still smiles to himself every time he thinks of it. Zadok would soon learn that Ahmed was a man to be taken very seriously. In so doing he would also learn why his father had a higher rank in the Supreme Council than his Uncle David.

Every other week Zadok would ride to the country and spend time with Rachel and Ambra. He had built a house in the Village of Joshua which saved him a half days ride to be with his family. It was still strange not having his grandparents there. Time has a way a healing all wounds. Zadok was discovering that not even time can remove the scars of a loss felt so deep.

Life for Zadok during this period was rather routine and uneventful. Days rolled into weeks and weeks into months. To say that there would be a time in which he wished for these good old days is expected. Then again, you would not have much to write about if things were going to remain routine and uneventful.

Ahmed In The Country

Strangely, before one of his visits back to see Rachel and Ambra, Zadok's father suggested that he take Ahmed with him. Zadok was a bit surprised; there would not be much for Ahmed to do in the country. He enjoyed Ahmed's company and it would be nice to have someone to ride together with. So off they went to the country. Ahmed talked non-stop all the way to the Village of Joshua. Zadok enjoyed every minute of it. Ahmed was full of tales. At times Zadok did not know which was true or, let's say, less true.

Rachel was nearing the term of delivery of the baby. Her Mother and two of her sisters were staying at the house when they arrived. Ahmed was made to feel like a family member and he fit right in as if he had always been there. One morning after the morning prayers and before breakfast, Ahmed asked Zadok to take a walk with him. He indicated that Zadok's father wanted him to show Zadok a few things. So they walked a distance out of the view of any of the surrounding houses.

They got to a point and Ahmed unfolded a leather case containing different types of knives. "Don't be alarmed," he said with a smile. "Your father wanted me to teach you how to use these," he said. "Why? I already know how to use a knife," said Zadok. "No, not these, these are not knifes. These are Sakeens," said Ahmed. Somewhat playfully Zadok replied, "They look like knives to me." Ahmed looked Zadok straight in the eye with a coldness that was bone chilling and said, "Sakeens are the tools of an assassin." Zadok was dumbfounded. "You are about to begin some very dangerous work. You are going to need all of the skills you can call on. You may never need these but, it is better to have and not need. Then to need and not have," said Ahmed. Then the lessons began.

They stayed in the country for three weeks. Each day Ahmed spent the better of it teaching Zadok the many ways to kill a man with or without a knife. Zadok was well trained in how to use his shepherd's staff as a defensive and offensive weapon. Ahmed had opened an entirely new world to him that would take years to master. Ahmed was an excellent teacher.

One day after the noon day break and a resumption of training, a servant came running to tell Zadok that the baby was coming. Zadok and Ahmed rushed back to the house to hear the cries of his new baby girl. They had cleaned her and handed her to her proud father. The baby stopped crying and stared at Zadok. Zadok rocking the baby showed her to Ahmed. Ahmed called her

Malika which in the language of his people meant Queen. Zadok loved the sound of the name and so her name became Malika. Ahmed was very pleased.

The Night Visitor

Back in the city Zadok's training continued discreetly. Every day without exception he would spend time with Ahmed learning something new or practicing something previously taught. He was also becoming more comfortable with his understanding of the many languages spoken in the city. At times during a conversation words from three or four different languages could be used. He was also spending less time with his cousins to their relief.

While in the city he stayed at his parent's home. Having grown up in his grandparents' home this was the first time that he actually lived with his parents. He got the chance to get to know his three brothers and two sisters. Zadok was the oldest and they all looked up to him and were very proud of him. They were all too young to work in the business but they were eager to spend as much time at the business as allowed. They had private tutors as was the custom of the well to do in the city. Zadok, having studied to be a priest, took charge of their religious instructions. He taught both his brothers and sisters and the sibling bonds were strengthened as a result.

From time to time Zadok's father would receive a late visitor. This person, Zadok assumed was always the same one who would visit long after everyone in the household was asleep. Within a day or two of the appearance of the Night Visitor, as Zadok would think of him, Aaron and Ahmed would be away for a few days or more. After one such trip to Merv, Zadok's father was brought back to the house by Ahmed severely injured. The story was that he got kicked by a horse. Zadok saw the wound and knew instantly what caused the near fatal injury. It was no horse. His father recovered from the injury but, he was never the same afterward. He had difficulty both walking and sitting for long periods until his last days.

Chapter 14

Signs, Symbols and Understanding

(Thoughts Of A.B. Naas)

Signs and Symbol as you are well accustomed to by now, can be used as an effective means of communication. Are not the letters you are writing put together as words to represent to the mind the signs and symbols comprising thought? Oh, I guess I should answer that in light of the fact that I am writing this story. The answer is yes. Which is better the word or that which the word represents? In most cases, that which the word represents. However, the words can serve as a symbol but not a substitute. For example the word ocean is no substitute for seeing one. This applies to both those things greater or smaller.

The tangible described in words is difficult enough. The intangible at times are nearly impossible to put into words. For those who have experienced it, how can the word "peace" come close to having it? What about the word "love" to the gift of sharing it? This last one, what justices can the two words "pure joy" do to one having experienced it? The intangible, I repeat, at times is nearly impossible to understand but, still we try.

Understanding is the objective that signs, symbols and words are meant to communicate (more often than not). But what does it mean to understand? There are several words in the Semitic languages used for understand. One of them translates best in the language you are reading is "door." There are some doors where the only understanding that you need or want, is for them to remain labeled and closed. There can be many reasons why you don't want to really know what is behind the door with the label. For now it is sufficient to mention such doors do exist. If the time and space that we are allowed includes this as a topic for my thoughts. We will come back to this.

There is another type of understanding where you want to know what is behind the door with the label. So you open the door and stand in the doorway. There is a perspective that is gained by just looking into the room. There is a perspective gained by walking into the room and examining its contents.

One way to describe having complete understanding would be the equivalents of standing in the center of a room suspended half way between the ceiling and the floor. Now imagine being able to comprehend everything in the room from a 360° perspective at the same time. (We will save the meaning of total understanding for another time).

There is another word in the Semitic languages that describes understanding as to comprehend as if to reach out and touch without doing so. However, signs, symbols and words can also be used almost equally as effect to impart misunderstanding. Now what does this have to do with where we are now in this story? Come let me shine some light on it...

Chapter 15

The Ebonites

The observers of the "Messiah" Movement, specifically those that followed the teachings of the Messiah, were called Ebonites. The term itself was possibly a pejorative one as used by some. However, at its root means is the word meaning the poor. Those that called the Followers of the Messiah Ebonites as an uncomplimentary term were the Pharisees. The Pharisees were rich and profited greatly from the Roman occupation. The Ebonites suffered greatly and were no friends to either the Romans or the Pharisees. The Ebonites were not passive and were preparing for war with the Romans.

The leaders of the Ebonites knew that an armed conflict with the Romans was inevitable. It was simply a matter of time. The Romans still believed that they killed the "Messiah" Joshua. Two years and running there were still people reporting that they had seen this Joshua. One such person you have already been introduced to; not by name, but by profession. Remember the Tax Collector at the beginning of this Saga? He and Zadok will cross paths many times. As a matter of fact he will have an entire section of these Chronicles to tell his story. We shall get to him in due time and space if allows.

It is often the case that a martyr can be more influential in death than they ever could be in life. The death of the "Messiah," real or imagined, only added to the problems of the Roman occupation. His movement grew well beyond their ability to contain it. But what was this movement about? Essentially, it was a re-dedication to the Mosaic Laws, a lessening of some of the restrictions, and an unwavering commitment to the poor and oppressed.

Explicit in His teachings, directed to the Children of Israel, was a re-dedication to the Mosaic Laws. In Palestine the primary occupants of this land were the Children of Israel. The focal point of the life of the Children of Israel was the Temple of Solomon. The Romans not only appointed the King of the Children of Israel but also the High priest of the Temple of Solomon. This was totally unacceptable to the Ebonites. It was also unacceptable to the overwhelming majority of the Children of Israel, be they Ebonites or not.

The unwavering commitment to the poor and oppressed was far more than lip service. As you will see these men and women numbering into the thousands were far more militant than they have been portrayed elsewhere. There is a reason for that, as well. However, those reason you will have to discover for yourself. Remember? If not remember this, I will only show you what is there, or theirs?

Palestine

It has now been nearly three years since Zadok and his father first visited the City of David in Palestine. Things have progressed much faster than they or anyone could have planned. To begin with the visit to Fars by James, son of Joseph, was completely unanticipated. It was not necessary to return to the City of David as soon as they had planned. Remember Eber, son of Caleb, the brother of Joshua? He would come to Fars once every six months or so to discuss any business related issues.

Murad and Luqman of the Axum people handled the business of the family related to the Caravans in Palestine. They were part of a network of people working for Aaron in each place of importance to the family business. In addition to the flow of money and safety of the Caravans to and from Fars they also managed the flow of information. Zadok would soon learn that information at times is more important than money.

Among the many things reported back to Fars was the condition of the Children of Israel under Roman occupation. The Roman repression was brutal and unforgiving. However, the Romans had never encountered a people quite like the Children of Israel. To be sure they had conquered and subjugated many other people, however, the people of Palestine; or what was sometimes called the Ehudi Province, were different. The Romans had never conquered a people so wedded to a land. They had never conquered a people so wedded to the focal point of their religious devotion, and they never would.

The overwhelming majority of the people hated the presence of the Romans. No occupation can be successful over an extended period without help from among the indigenous people. The Roman occupation of Ehudi Province was aided by the Pharisees. The Pharisees were part of the Children of Israel. However, the vision of the Pharisees was far different than that of the "Messiah" and his followers.

It was from among the Pharisees that the Romans picked a King for the Ehudi People. In addition the Romans designated the High priest for the Temple of Solomon from among this group. In time the power and importance of the Pharisees would grow. It would grow to the point that it would be a reasonable question to ask, "Who was really in charge, the Pharisees or the Romans?" Once again, we are getting ahead of ourselves so let's return.

The dynamics and history of the Ehudi People in Palestine where such that there was going to be a war with the Romans. In actuality the war had already begun. This was the assessment presented by Luqman and Murad and their team of Spotters. Who are the Spotters? I am glad you asked. For context we will say that without the Spotters the House of Joseph would have remained Shepherds and Farmers.

Spotters

Servants are the apparently mindless individuals always floating around the rich doing things that the rich are too rich to do. They are always underpaid and under-appreciated and if they had any brains at all; well, they would not be servants. Such was the thinking of many of the rich and far too wealthy concerning servants.

To those looking at these same individuals with a different pair of eyes; these same individuals are good candidates to become Spotters. Spotters can go where no one else can go. They can see what no one else can see. Most important of all they can hear what no one else was meant to hear. These things, when put together, made them worth their weight in gold. They also have the added advantage of being able to do all of the above again, and again, and again. Thus is the value of a Spotter.

Ahmed and his people were always in search of candidates to become Spotters. The best prospects were those who were slaves or servants but, who did not want to be. If they could do a good enough job as a Spotter, then they would be bought and set free. Many would then come and work for the business doing various jobs for pay. Some were inclined to do other types of work, while paid to do whatever they did. There were those who would have paid to do certain types of jobs. It was those you had to keep an eye on. Sometimes they were too zealous in the execution of their assignments.

Thou Shall Not Murder

(or was that kill?)

It would be difficult to be more explicit. However, is it murder when you kill to protect your family? What about your extended family? What about your tribe? Assume that the threat is not immediate but a potential one; is it murder then? These are no longer theoretical arguments for Zadok. The night visitor has come and gone. His father is no longer in a position to address issues of "prime importance." An issue of "prime importance" is what the Elders called it when there is a threat against the House of Joseph. Not just any threat, but a threat where the only solution is to remove the threat by killing it.

For Ahmed this was an issue that was reconciled long ago. For Zadok who had never killed a human being and now was about to kill three; well, for him it was far more than an academic question. But we are getting ahead of ourselves in as much as that is possible on the circle that is time. I guess it would be helpful if we walked back a bit on this circle and try and understand a little more. Yes, we need to understand a little more as to how and why Zadok has come to this place. Not just the place where this deed will be done. We need to understand how he answered those questions within his, let us agree to say - soul.

In "The Beginning" 2

Three weeks ago Zadok's father asked him to sit with him a while in the garden to talk. It was late and Zadok was a bit tired but the opportunity to spend some alone time with his father was welcomed. He had not done that since they returned from the City of David. His father positioned himself in his favorite garden chair and began, what Zadok now viewed as, a wind up to something important. He did not know what it was but, as he sat on the edge of his chair, his father told him to set back and relax. Zadok did as he was told, as much as he could, and waited for his father to speak.

"My son the duties of our family have always been great," he said. Almost as if to exhale, the entire statement and in making it was about to shift some gigantic burden on to Zadok. Communicated with that was also a great reluctance and hesitancy in what he was about to say and do. He went on to talk about the history of the family beginning with their ancestor the Messenger Joseph. For the very first time his father gave him information about his ancestors that no one had ever shared with him.

His beloved grandfather had, of course, drilled into his head his lineage extending all the way back to father Abraham. Actually, if pushed, he could remember what his grandfather taught him regarding his linage back to Adam. The hour was late and what his father was now sharing with him was far more interesting. Much like the time after his encounter with the Roman soldier, his body's cries for rest had been put to rest. Ancestor after ancestor his father listed the deeds and sacrifices of those, in his bloodline, had made. The manner in which he did this was as if he were reading from a scroll. Neither of them noticed, but as his father spoke they both seemed to draw strength and inspiration from his father's words. Possibly yet, in another way, like father like Son.

Finally, his father got to his grandfather. It turns out that his grandfather, if he had been alive, would have been one of the seven Elders of the Supreme-Council. His grandfather had earned Six Colors. This was the highest rank ever achieved thus far by anyone in the House of Joseph. As his father paused and let the tears flow freely from his eyes; Zadok, not caught up in the emotions of the moment, thought back to the meeting of the

Supreme-Council. There were four tiers not including the ground level. Could there be a connection? Would it have been possible for his grandfather to occupy the ground level or tier alone?

As his father collected himself Zadok commented from his heart how much he too missed both his grandparents. His father began to tell the story of his grandfather. Unknown to Zadok, his grandfather began and finished his studies to be a priest rather late in life. This was long after he had married and began his own family. His grandfather, like his father before him, was trained as a servant to deal with "Issues of Prime Importance." His father did not go into details but you could see the added erectness to his posture when he added, "He was the Chief and Supreme Servant."

Zadok sat there with his mouth open and his eyes opened comparatively wider as he tried to process this information.   His father seeming not to notice, or possibly ignoring his son's reaction, continued, "My Days as a Servant of Issues of Prime Importance are over" he said as his shoulders seemed to slump. "Your Days are about to begin," he said as he appeared to regain his erect posture. "It had been my hope to have been with you as my father was with me on my first assignment," he said. "That wish and dream of mine will not be realized. For me to attempt to do that would put us both in danger. This is your final lesson before you begin your assignment. Know your limitations," with that there was a long period of silence. The silence was broken when the night visitor and Ahmed entered the garden and laid out the assignment and plan.

Two Targets

The Governor of Merv was a Nephew to the King. This Governor hated, with a passion, the Children of Israel. His, whose chosen, name was Epiphanes; he was a student of history. He thought of himself as god manifested in man. The idea that the Children of Israel had of a Deity superior to him, the sovereign, was completely offensive to him. He believed that his laws, and only his laws, should be recognized by his subjects. In so far as the Children of Israel were his subject. The Governor felt that they should have no other god before him.

The family business of the House of Joseph was built trading on the Silk Road. Trade along this route represents nearly 80 percent of the income needed to support the House of Joseph in Persia and all of its projects. This new Governor had no idea as to the size and importance of this business to the House of Joseph. He only understood that it all flowed through the Province he now controlled.

The calculated risk of killing a Governor carried with it dangers that were great. There could also be unintended consequences. If murder was suspected in the death of a Governor the ramification could lead in any direction. Possibly even back to the House of Joseph. If that is what had to be done so be it, however there were other targets available than could be more impactful. In addition, the removal of these targets would have other benefits as you shall soon see.

The Governor Epiphanes had inserted a Broker of his choosing to trade with the House of Joseph on all trades coming through his Province. The Governor's Broker's objective was to squeeze the profits from the House of Joseph to nothing or less, if possible. It turns out the Broker had a sexual perversion that on occasion took him to a part of the city that was both dark and seedy. He would always have guards that accompanied him to a point to protection him. So he would be no easy target.

The Broker once removed could easily be replaced with someone even worse. So steps were taken to limit the field of potential replacements. The best prospect was a man they knew well from the Aimaq Tribe. The House of Joseph had done business with his tribe for years. He was powerful enough so that the Governor could not push him around too easily. In addition, he was open for making a little more Drachma so that the Governor would make a lot less. The House of Joseph calculated that the status quo of profitability would be maintained if not improved just a little.

Killing the Broker was not enough. They had to also start a conflict on the border away from the Silk Road. This would ensure that the Governor's attention would be directed at more pressing matters. Of the two targets this second one would be more difficult. They had decided to create a conflict between two rival tribes. A conflict too big could engulf the entire region and lead to a war.

As the plan was explained to Zadok there seemed to be an emotional element lurking just beneath the surface directed at this second target. This motive, whatever it was, existed with his father, Ahmed, and the night visitor. Zadok saw clearly that this added motivation for removing this second target was there. No time to think of that now. He had to focus.

The night visitor concluded his presentation before the Morning Prayer. There were many questions and modifications to the plan before the consensus was articulated by Ahmed. The three of them nodded their acceptance of Ahmed's summary of action. They collectively turned to Zadok. Prior to that point he was more of a spectator. He neither asked a question for clarity or justification. This, after all, was his very first mission. "Do you understand?" his father questioned. As if that was not enough Ahmed asked, "Do you have any questions?" Zadok responded to both by saying, "Yes, I understand and no I have no questions." Ahmed and Aaron looked at each other not knowing what to say do or express.

The four of them said their morning's prayers together. Ahmed and the night visitor left shortly afterward. They all needed time to rest.

First Things First

Following the plan, Ahmed and Zadok took the steps to first create the conflict between the two tribes. There were two young people from these tribes who had caught each other's eyes. There was a blossoming attraction between the two. It was the job of the night visitor and his network of other Spotters to know such things. The father of the boy was the Chief of the Herati Tribe. The Herati Tribe, if they sold all that they owned, could not afford the dower for the girl. Her father was a very wealthy cattle herder from the Aimaq Tribe. She would not come cheap.

Zadok and Ahmed's assignment was to kidnap the girl and sell her to slavers. Her youth and beauty would bring a very handsome price. They were not interested in the money but, they took it. Their only interest was to create conflict and confusion. Unfortunately, two of her guards would have to be killed in order to kidnap her and send her away. So it had to be.

As for the young man he was to be killed by the traditional weapon (a knife) carried in the waistband of young men from the girls tribe. Zadok was trained to expect the unexpected. Zadok could not have imagined that as he approached the young man; he was waving to him as if he knew him on that lonely road. The young man smiled at him in the same manner as his friend Simon. Zadok will never forget the look on the young man face as he slit his throat. The young man whose name Zadok did not know, tried to ask a question. There was just a gurgling sound as the light went out of his eyes and he died.

Thus far, everything had gone just as the night visitor planned. The death of the young man and the missing girl would flame tribal tensions. There could very well be a war if the Governor did not have the skills to place a lid on this brew. Over the next several days there were many arguments by each tribe as what to do next. The young man is dead. Where is the girl? Clearly she did not run away with the young man? Was there another young man? Is he responsible for killing their young man? They had to bring in other tribal members. They even had to send for the Governor to prevent an all-out war. Mission accomplished.

By the time the Governor arrived in the Province, the young lady was well on her way to a new life. She would be in a land beautiful in a different way than her own but still not hers. She would never see her relatives or land again. One day many years from now (for her) she will strain to remember the name of a boy that she was once fond of as a young girl. She will be surrounded by her children and their children and their children. The love she feels for them causes all thoughts of a boy whose name she could not recall to vanish as a potential thought. Until the next time when that which is, is not that which could have been, crosses her mind...

The Governor's Broker

The Governor of Merv was called away to deal with the tribal crisis. This was a signal to the Governor's designated broker that it was a time to visit the dark side. This broker could only feed his perversion among the extremely poor and needy. In the back alleys where they lived he could pay for what he wanted and walk away when finished and not look back. The broker had talked a few of his contemporaries and underlings into testing his delights out along with him. He extended his invitations carefully; scandals are always good for blackmail. How such people identify one another shall always be a mystery to us. The Governor's broker was now seen as a rising star. The higher the star, the more inclined people were to overlook some deeds. Most declined politely but, there were a few that would join him seeking favor and perversity. Unfortunately, for all that accompanied him there would be no happy ending.

The Governor's broker, embolden by his position, had taken the liberty of hosting a dinner at the Governor's court. It was completely and totally improper for the broker to act as such. The Governor did not give him permission to do so and would not if asked. The broker calculated that the Governor was in such a rush to get to the outer province of Merv, that he had not canceled the dinner. He went on to assume the role as the host because he knew that no one would challenge him. About that he was correct; no one did challenge him. The guests departed and the broker and his four companions prepared themselves from the second part of their entertainment.

Zadok and Ahmed slipped back into town and met the Spotters as agreed. It had taken the two of them four days to make a trip that should have taken a day and a half at most. The Spotters had made all of the arrangements required by Zadok and Ahmed. They decided to get a little rest. It was still a few hours before night fall and after they carried out their assignment they would leave the city immediately.

Time To Go

Ahmed shook Zadok lightly and he sat straight up as if pushed up by a spring. He swung his legs over to the edge of the bed. Without hesitating he walked over to the picture filled with water and the basin. He took a drink of water before pouring the rest of it into the basin. There he began to wash up as much as he could in this dark, damp and smelly room. He would later complain about the room a bit to Ahmed. Ahmed would laugh and tell him of places that he and his father had to stay. As Zadok washed, he thought of Rachael and his girls. Rachael was pregnant again. This time he wanted a boy. He loved his daughters but, he wanted a son.

The Spotter had already left to establish his alibi. Not that he needed one but, you can never be too cautious in this line of work. Zadok and Ahmed made their way to the place that the broker would be in a few hours. They traveled by roof top in the dark another precaution as was said before; you can never be too careful. They entered the converted warehouse through the rafters and waited in the shadows and darkness above.

Down below was Hell, which is the only way Zadok could describe what he did not want to see. Every type of sexual perversion unimaginable was occurring below him. Some of the people he wanted to rescue. Some he wanted to kill for the things that he saw them enjoying. The most horrible thing that he saw was more than a few of his people as both spectators and participants in the den of vice and sin.

Zadok began to sweat profusely. He sweats so profusely that the sweat ran down his face as if he had just come in from a heavy rain. Ahmed became concerned that the anxiety Zadok was experiencing would put the mission in jeopardy. Zadok assured him that he would be ok by showing him the steadiness of his hand. It was not long before the target, with his guest, came in a side door.

The broker was well familiar with the person who let him in, as he slipped a few coins into his hand. If it had been possible to bend over double, the host would have done so gladly. More coins from the broker for the extra effort of course. The broker spoke briefly to the host and pointed to his three companions as the Host nodded none stop. The Host spoke to the three and ushered the Broker into a private room.

There were no ceilings on any of the room. The night sky provided ventilation and instant cooling air against the accumulated heat of any room. The incense burning just at head level warned any insect of instant suffocation should they try and seek a meal from so much unclothed flesh. Ahmed pointed to the broker indicating that he wanted Zadok to take care of him. Ahmed would take care of whatever else had to be taken care of for the evening.

Zadok moved effortlessly from rafter to rafter seeming like the smoke rising and being carried by the wind. He was there, then not there, if anyone had been curious enough to look up to see. The Broker had disrobed and was lying face down on a table at the center of a windowless room. As Zadok moved in on the Broker, a young girl came into the room covering him in towels.

As she left, Zadok was in position to do exactly what he came there to do. He reeled what could best be described as an ax into place. Once positioned, he let it drop on its own weight. The Broker neither heard nor saw it coming. When it landed it severed the Broker's neck almost in two. He died there wrapped in towels rapidly becoming soaked with his blood with a strange curious look on his face. It almost looked like he was about to say, "I wonder what?"

The ax was attached to a chain that allowed Zadok to reel the ax back to him. There was a trail of blood. He had hoped by the time anyone noticed it he would be back in the Village of Joshua enjoying Rachel and the girls. He got the ax and began moving back up and through the rafters to make his escape. Thus far everything had gone according to plan. He could now see that Ahmed was also moving to the place of their escape. Then they heard a scream louder than all the other noises. There was the sound of glass breaking and more screams.

The News From Merv

Zadok and Ahmed had been in Fars for about a week when news of the great fire in the city of Merv came. The fire was started in a seedy gritty part of the city known for nothing good. It was said that as many as two thousand people were killed during the fire. Hundreds, if not thousands more died as a result of civil unrest, looting, rape, robbery, and murder.

The Governor of Merv was away dealing with another problem when the fire occurred. He had the entire army garrison with him. So there was no law and order to either contain the fire or the people. This did not sit well with the King.

Three of Zadok's cousins were in the city of Merv, as well; they were expected back shortly. They were expected to have more news of the fire when they returned. As days rolled into weeks and weeks into months the cousins never showed up. They never came. It was said, "They must have been a victim of foul play!" Whether they were victims of foul play or died at the place of the fire, no one; I repeat, no one will ever know for sure.

Chapter 16

Zadok Speaks To Zadok

This was Zadok's first mission. He had slit the throat of a man he did not know that reminded him of his friend Simon. He killed a man he did not know at the last place where anyone would want to die. In the process he possibly indirectly helped kill thousands of other people. Not to mention he destroyed almost half of a city - and that poor girl Ahmed and the Spotters (he presumed) kidnapped. Why did he participate in all of this again? He thought to himself looking for rationalization. Zadok was deeply troubled with no one to talk to.

In his heart of hearts, for the first time possibly, he began to ask questions about what others were instructing him to do. Zadok did not think of himself as a blind follower. Many have commented on his intellect. He took it for granted that since others thought of him as being smart, he was smart. Where was his smartness when he did not question his orders to go kill a couple of people? If the people that gave him those orders were so smart, why did they not anticipate the fire that killed so many people? Accidents happen all the time but, did he cause the accident by killing the Broker? Maybe the accident was caused by Ahmed; he killed some people too! If so, is he any less to blame? What if Ahmed went there to cause the fire? Is he any less to blame?

These questions were rattling around in Zadok's head when he informed his Uncle David that he wanted to complete his training to become a priest. His uncle looked at him surprised and asked, "Why? I want you to work with your father." Zadok responded, "Yes, I know but, I want to finish what I started with grandfather." For a moment David hesitated, he must have thought of his father. He then said, "You can complete your training with me." "Good," said Zadok, "When can we start?" "We can start after the Sabbath." "Thanks," said Zadok. The two of them seemed to avoid each other for the remainder of that week.

Needed In The City

Zadok was happy to be a student again. In a way it took his mind off of the unintended consequences of his first mission. He had been in the village for maybe six weeks when his father sent him a message that he was needed in the city. His heart sank. 'Needed in the city for what?' he thought. It could only mean one thing - another mission.

Zadok arrived in the city at midday of the following day. The hustle and bustle of city life he had almost forgotten. He wished that he could forget a lot more. What he did not forget was that he did not like the city or, for that matter, any city. He went straight to the house in that everyone would have been there for the midday rest. And so it was. He greeted everyone and they enjoyed a midday meal made by his mother. He was beginning to think that she could cook almost as good as his grandmother.

After the meal his father asks him to join him in the garden. They each took their seats in their usual chairs and his father began to speak without hesitation. "I am expecting a visitor tonight. I want you to wait up with me to hear what he has to say," his father said. "Don't know if I can do that father," Zadok heard himself say before he could close his mouth and be quiet. His father said, "Excuse me," as one would say upon hearing one's own language spoken by someone just learning to speak. "I said, I don't think I can," Zadok said again not backing down at all. "You have been called and you will answer the call. I will take my rest now and I will see you later." His father was not angry; there was a certain matter of fact nature about his statement. His statement left Zadok with the feeling of 'now that that is settled let us move on.' And so they did.

Artifacts

Back in Merv there were a certain number of personal artifacts found in the rubble that belonged to members of the Children of Israel. In relationship to where they were found, the wearers of these artifacts had to be very close to the origin of the fire. This started tongues to wagging. "You know those people start trouble wherever they go," one said. "I would not be surprised if they burned the entire place down so that they could buy it cheap," said another. "They think that they are better than everyone," they continued.

Several members of the Children of Israel were beaten on the street. More than a few had their shops looted in broad daylight by the youth. Their neighbors and fellow shopkeepers just looked on. To them it was a form of afternoon entertainment. The Governor who was splitting his time between the city and keeping the tribes to the north from going to war was not the least bit concerned. Something had to be done and quick.

A decision was made to kill two members of each of the major tribes in the city. In this way, if it were done properly, they would be too busy fighting each other, thus they would forget about the Children of Israel. Zadok, with his new found critical thinking skills, thought that this was the dumbest plan possible. However, there was no appeal system. His mission was to complete the mission or to die trying.

Once Again

Twelve days later Zadok and Ahmed were back in the city from his first mission. Zadok had come to view actions that you know are not right, but you do them anyway, as a crime against the soul. The smell of burnt wood and flesh was still in the air. He would learn that anyone that has ever smelled burnt human flesh or hair would never forget the smell.

The two targets were picked. They were both young men. A bit unbridled and hot headed. There had been a major fight between the two tribes not more than a week ago. So, killing one tribal member and making the injury of the other look like it came from the one killed. This should be all that was needed to ignite a fire in search of a spark. Both targets drank heavily and they were each at opposite ends of town. The major challenge for Ahmed and Zadok was to not be seen by anyone. All Zadok, Ahmed, and the two Spotters had to do was wait for the opportunity.

The opportunity for Ahmed came early. His target came out of the drinking establishment to relieve himself. Ahmed moved silently to the door of the outhouse. As his target finished his business and stepped out of the outhouse. Ahmed looked around before grabbing him by his chin. And with a quick jerk he broke the young man's neck. The target dropped as if the strings of a Puppet Marionette had been cut. Ahmed moved so quickly it is doubtful the target had the time to blink his eyes twice. Ahmed dragged him to the back of the outhouse completely out of sight. He then went to check on Zadok.

Zadok and his spotter were still waiting when Ahmed arrived. Ahmed looked at Zadok with great concern. The night was cool. Some would say it was actually cold. There was Zadok standing in the shadows wet with sweat from head to toe. Ahmed said, "What do you plan to do, drown your target in your sweat?" They all laughed quietly, reducing for the moment the anxiety Zadok felt. The anxiety quickly returned with a little more to add. The target, with two male companions, was emerging from the drinking establishment. This made things three times as complicated.

As the target walked with his companions Ahmed, Zadok, and the two spotters followed. The target with his companions were taking their time and walking towards the stables. Ahmed said, "We will have to take all three." Zadok tried to question the decision. Unfortunately he could not find the words. He felt that all of his fluids had been converted to sweat. The only sound he could make with his mouth was a dry smacking noise.

Ahmed told Zadok that once inside the stable he would take the two on the right. All Zadok had to do is to cut the throat of the target. The two Spotters looked at each other awaiting instructions. Ahmed turned to them and said, "Once these three are down take a wagon from the stable and pick up the body behind the drinking establishment." With that they quickened their steps so as to arrive at the stables nearly at the same time as the targets.

The stable was unattended. This was a break for Zadok. Ahmed would not have had any problem adding another body to the list. The targets noticed them shortly before they got to the stables. Zadok, Ahmed and the Spotters began talking among themselves and acting as if they had even more to drink than the targets. The targets quickly dismissed them as being harmless.

The targets entered the stable first. Within three steps Ahmed entered and Zadok was just a step behind him. The Spotters stayed on the outside. On the outside all that was heard was one heavy thing falling to the ground. Then there was the sound of a second heavy object falling to the ground. A moment later there was an inaudible sound and then the third heavy object fell to the ground. Ahmed said just loud enough for the Spotters to hear, "Come in and get the wagon." Ahmed instructed them not to ride too quickly or too slowly. He told them exactly where he had hid the body. He and Zadok pulled the three bodies out of sight.

Before too much time had passed for them to become concerned, the two Spotters were back with the body. Ahmed told them to wait outside out of sight and let him know if anyone was coming. He told Zadok where he wanted him to place the other three corpses. As Zadok was moving the first body he noticed that Ahmed was hacking, cutting and mutilating the body of the corpse taken from the wagon. Zadok yelled, "WHAT ARE YOU DOING!" Ahmed looked at him shocked. He stopped walked over to Zadok with weapon in hand. Zadok noticed this and dropped the corpse and took out his two favorite weapons. Ahmed stopped well short of Zadok and said, "We have to make this look like this one guy put up a great fight against these three. That will inflame the passions on both sides. Do what I asked you to do quickly. I want to get as far away from this place as soon as we can."

Zadok did what he was told. There were no further incidences. The spotters disappeared. Zadok and Ahmed were back in Fars within two days. During the entire journey back not a word was spoken between the two. Mission accomplished and objective achieved.

Lots Of Priests

News of the Visitors to Fars spread throughout the entire Israeli Community located in the Parthian Empire. A meeting was called of all the leading priests in the empire. "Now let me see if I got this right. The "Messiah" came, but, had to go away, but, he will be back. In the meantime we are supposed to lay a foundation for a New Messenger. His name will be Praiseworthy and he will not speak in his own name. In addition you want me to tell my people to give the Temple all of their wealth so that they can give it to the poor. Hold on, wait - I am not finished. You also want us to help the Disciples of the

"Messiah" in their war against the Romans." The priest that made these sarcastic remarks was not from Fars but it did not matter. He was expressing the sentiments of most of the 500 or more priest that had gathered from around the Parthian Empire.

News had gotten out that not only has the "Messiah" appeared in Palestine. He has sent representative to Fars Province. There, in Fars Province, he had presented proof of his authority. The Members of the Supreme-Council were under oath not to discuss anything that occurred or was said at any Supreme-Council meeting. All that they would say is that they saw the proof and they are convinced. This was not going to be enough for most of the priests attending the conference that did not see the "clear evidence" themselves.

The priest Abraham from the city in Shiraz was probably not the best one to make a presentation that was so important. The priest Abraham was sweaty and he spoke with a nasal tone. He was also very short. The fact that he darted his head around looking for someone; anyone with a friendly face did not help. This was going to be a hard sell. Too hard a sell for the priest Abraham to make alone and no one came to his aide. Trying as best he could, the priest Abraham could not communicate his feeling and understanding about the "Messiah" and the Ebonites that followed him.

What became apparent to some was that things were about to change for not only the House of Joseph but all of the Children of Israel. Anyone with ambition, and there was plenty of ambition in that room, wanted to be at the top when these changes came about. Poor priest Abraham thought that he would solidify his position at the top by being the first to learn and teach the New Covenant. His grasp fell well short of his reach. He felt it and knew it as everyone else in the room did also.

The Delegation

It was decided that a delegation of seven would be sent to the City of David. Zadok and his Uncle David would lead the delegation. Five others were chosen based on their power and authority in relationship to all the others. Zadok sensed that his Uncle David would rather not have him as part of the delegation. He put that aside for the moment, knowing it was real, but he wanted to consider the other five that would be going to Palestine.

Among the delegation was a priest by the name Jbezan who claimed to be an Amonite. Jbezan was more

Greek than he was Israeli in his clothing, speech, and disposition. It was hard for Zadok to understand why he would even want to go on such a mission. Zadok would keep an eye on him. The two priests Barak and Gideon were the kind of priests his grandfather would have approved. They too looked suspiciously at the priest Jbezan. The priests Eli and Shamgar were clearly very knowledgeable. Conversely, about worldly things they appeared to be clueless. If for nothing more than academic reasons they would be good to have on this mission.

Zadok agreed to make the arrangement so that they could each get into Palestine with the least amount of trouble. This would be easy for him in light of the business his family was now doing with Tobiad and Cousin Eber. The priest Jbezan indicated that he would make his own arrangements. He had friends there in the City of David. They would meet him and get him past the Romans. It was noted by Zadok that he did not offer to extend these arrangement to anyone else.

Zadok was beginning to wonder if this man was a spy; but a spy for whom? It did not matter Zadok thought. If he was a spy then... He caught himself. That was not his decision to make.

Politician

On the way to the City of David there was much to consider. For Zadok the subject of Politics preoccupied his mind. "Politics is the art and or science of getting people to do more than they would do otherwise." At least this was Zadok's grandfather definition of Politics. So, by way of extension a politician was a person that had the ability to get people to do these things. In Zadok's mind he was struggling with the concept of politicians did only what they were allowed to do by the people. Zadok found this discussion inside of his head far more interesting than the one that Uncle David and the four priests were having. To him they were having a 'How many Angels can dance on the head of a pin,' debate. This is how his grandfather would have categorized the discussion about theoretical issues than are not resolvable.

They had been riding for two days and should catch up with the caravan headed for Palestine in another day or so. Zadok was riding slightly ahead of the others. He was lost in thought with his own considerations. The Ebonites, by all reports, has continued to grow to the dismay of the Royal family, those Israelis that supported them, and the Romans. Sooner or later there will be a war for the City of David. The Ebonites, growing in strength daily, will have to direct that power at something. It is the people that empower the politicians. Like it or not James, son of Joseph, was now a politician. If he was not before, he is certainly one now. What do the people want? They want the City of David, the Temple, and to be relieved of the burden of debt they had been forced into. The individuals and groups that have these things now are not going to willing hand them over without a fight. About that Zadok was certain.

Now here he is a part of a delegation to discover the truth about the "Messiah." "Why am I here?" he said loud enough for the others to hear. "When you get tired of talking to yourself come back here and give us some of your wisdom." He knew not who said this, but they all laughed loudly. Zadok did not have to be convinced about anything concerning the "Messiah." It has been five children, (Rachel is pregnant again), too many killings to want to count, the loss of his grandparents, and 15 years. He was there because someone with an agenda other than his wanted him there. It certainly was not his Uncle David. "Politics!" Zadok said with disdain. He realized that once again someone else was pulling his strings. He did not know why? He only knew that he did not like it.

People

They caught up with the caravan just before it reached the first Roman Checkpoint. Zadok had all the priests change into clothing more befitting business people. With a few words and coins they passed through the checkpoint without any delay. It seemed to Zadok that there were Roman patrols everywhere. It had been 15 years since his last visit to Palestine. Things had changed dramatically.

Their business had grown significantly there in the City of David over the years. The decision was made to build a modest, by Persian standards, compound for themselves. Zadok's room in the compound was spacious, cool, and comfortable. This is the first time that he had seen this space built for him. He took a tour of the compound after resting and freshening up and bumped into his Uncle David doing the same.

"This is all very nice," he said to Zadok. Zadok replied, "I am glad you like it." Zadok was coming down the stairs as Uncle David was walking across the courtyard. "I see your room is on the second level," his Uncle said. "Would you mind if I saw your room?" "Of course not, be my guest," Zadok said, not thinking anything of the request. Which was just as well, he will have a lot of time to think about the reaction.

Zadok walked with his uncle through a courtyard on the second level directly to his room. From the reaction of his Uncle David you would have thought that Zadok's room was the Royal Palace of some great King. "You have all of this and you have me down with the servants and farm animals!" his uncle yelled. "I am your priest, I am your Teacher, I am your uncle and the leader of this family, and you show me no respect!" His uncle screamed while standing there just in side of the doorway.

When his uncle began to yell and before he had a chance to understand what he was saying, Zadok pivoted and crouched while grabbing his Sakeens all in one fluid motion. When he turned, all that was there was his Uncle David. His Uncle David was shaking from his anger; eyes bloodshot, and though his skin was brown it appeared that it had been drained of all blood.

Zadok thought for a moment, "Will these shocks and surprises of my life never cease?" Then he said, "Uncle David, I have never been here before. I had nothing to do with which room you got. Nor, for what it is worth, which room that I got. We will get you another room, and if we can't, you can have this one and I will take yours." If only he had stopped there, "It really does not matter to me," he concluded. "Oh, now you are calling the lack of respect shown to me a trivial matter!" With that Uncle David turned walked out the room and slammed the door as he exited. Zadok stood there frozen trying to decide if what he thinks just happened really happened or did he imagine that it did.

Fifteen Years

After the incident with Uncle David, Zadok decided to go for a walk to check out the surroundings. He decided that he would speak to the attendant of their villa when he returned. This time, unlike the first time he was in the City of David, he carried no shepherd's staff. The concealed weapons he carried would do just fine if needed. There was really not much to see. All of the villas were contained behind gated walls with watch towers. In the watch towers were guards that spoke. He returned the greeting as a common courtesy. He walked in the center of the graveled road with his hands behind his back. This gave the impression that he was just out for a walk lost in thought. He really did not want to engage the guards or anyone else in conversation.

Fifteen years? Where did the time go? It had been fifteen years since he was last in the City of David. He was not sure if where he was could be considered still the City of David so far away. The entire area where the villa was located overlooked much of the city. He could actually see right into the heart of the city from almost anywhere along the hill side. He tried to remember if there were villas on this hillside fifteen years ago? He did not notice or could not remember.

Fifteen Years? So much has happened in just fifteen short years. Zadok was now thirty one. His father would soon turn forty five. An age that now seemed not so old to a man of thirty one. Zadok thought of his growing family. He smiled as he remembered each of them. His beloved wife Rachel; how he missed her so much when he was away. He had been away a lot over the last fifteen years. Most of the time away was spent with Ahmed doing what they had become so good at doing. When he was with or thought of Ahmed he thought of death.

Fifteen Years? Ambra would soon be fourteen. He would soon have to start thinking about a husband for her. No wait she's too young! He needed to think of something else. Yes, Malika she so much reminds him of his own mother. Let's see she will be thirteen soon. Then there was Joshua his son. He looked like and was headstrong like Zadok's beloved grandfather. If anyone had been looking at Zadok, they would have noticed that his eyes were a bit glassy.

Fifteen Years? His son Reuben they named after Rachel's father, a fact that he beamed about whenever his namesake was around. If he had been thinking they would have named him Aaron Ruben or Ruben Aaron. His mother, Ruth, put pressure on his wife and him to have another boy, so that they can name him Aaron.

Fifteen Years? They had secretly started to train members of the Ebonites in the art form of assassinations. James, son of Joseph, did not really like the idea. It was not so much that he had a problem with the idea that people would have to die. People had already died on both sides of the coming war. His issue was who decides who lives and who dies. In open warfare you have two sides pitted against one another. If you are on a battlefield you are there to either kill or be killed. Assassinations, someone or a group of people decide that a person or group of people should die. If it were James, the son of Joseph, making the decision - well not even the person being assassinated would be able to find fault with his judgment. He was known to be that just. Well maybe they would he thought with a chuckle but, in their heart of hearts, they would know that he was right.

Fifteen Years? He was now a priest. His grandfather would be proud. As his vision blurred again and this time the tears did flow. A priest of what he thought? The Old Covenant had been replaced with the New Covenant. With that thought he realized that was at the heart of so much that has happened over the last fifteen years. A number of priests in and around Fars had now trained to be Disciples of the New Covenant. The priests that have not trained are now secondary to those that have trained in the New Covenant. What was to be done with so many First Covenant priests; many of which were institutions themselves? What was he going to do as a priest? With that thought he ran out of road and headed back to the villa.

Surprise!

The walk back did not take him long. Then again since it was the same distance as the walk to the end of the road it took about the same time. Zadok's thoughts about the New Covenant priest versus the Old Covenant priest occupied his mind for the entire distance. Was it really supposed to be that way the New versus the Old? He thought not, as he reached his villa's gates. He remembered that he had to talk to the attendant about Uncle David's room. As he headed for the area that he thought the attendant would be in, he caught a glimpse of him in another section of the court yard. He changed direction and headed straight for him.

As Zadok reached him he noted that it always appeared to him that servants and employees always appeared to be busy doing something. Either they were cleaning what had already been cleaned or fixing that which was not broken. It was not that he minded but, why the act? Zadok had never known hunger, need, or servitude. So understanding why anyone once freed of such things would put on an act to stay free of such things was not within his grasps. Not yet, anyway, but maybe one day?

The attendant's whose name Zadok did not bother to remember greeted him as he approached. The attendant listened patiently as Zadok requested a different room for his uncle. No need to go into the whys and what for. He was a servant and Zadok expected him to make the change without delay. There were plenty of empty rooms. Zadok was rather shocked when the attendant said that he could not change Uncle David's room. Without hesitating he asked in an instinctive authoritarian manner, "And why not!?" Before, Zadok could take his next breath the attendant replied, "This note from your father instructed me not to change his room under any circumstances."

The note read just as the attendant said. Not that Zadok doubted that it would have. The note had to be read regardless. It contained the message with the seal of his father he could see and smell. His father's scented oils, and dyes wax provided by Ruben his father-in-law was evident. Stammering a bit he asked the attendant, "Where did you get this from?" The attendant replied, "From the man in the room next to yours." Zadok turned to go up to find out who and why this message was delivered. The attendant exhaled a sigh of relief, glad to pass the explanation of his refusal and the note to someone else.

Zadok has had enough of these manipulations. He could not confront his father until he returned to Fars. He intended to do just that when he returned. That would be the very first thing that he does. Zadok walked up the stairs thinking about just the right words to say. After all, Aaron was still his father. He had to be respectful. Zadok knocked on the door rather loudly. Knowing clearly that the person inside did not, could not have as much authority as he had. If it had been his father which he ruled out, there would be no need for a note with a seal. Zadok's mouth opened wide, his eyes comparatively wider. He recognized the person and the smile immediately when Ahmad opened the door and said, "As Salaam brother, I have been waiting for you. Come on in we need to talk."

Ahmed

(again)

As Zadok allowed Ahmed to lead him into the room by his arm. Ahmed made a mental note that Zadok was still too trusting. In Ahmed's mind Zadok should have at least looked around the room to see if anyone else was there. Zadok just stared at Ahmed completely shocked to see him. Ahmed made a mental note that he would have to talk to Zadok about this very soon. For now he had to get Zadok up to speed quickly. They were very far behind enemy lines. If things were not handled properly over the next few days neither of them would see home again.

As quickly as he could he lead Zadok to a chair and started to explain. He began by apologizing on behalf of

Aaron for keeping him in the dark so long. He spoke quietly and quickly. The distant cousin from Heron that invited Aaron to the City of David was a spy. Zadok had come to know Eber very well. The man was a pawn maybe, but, a spy? A moot point one way or the other, in light of everything else Ahmed had to say.

The banker Tobiad was a Pharisee. As such, he was a supporter of the Roman occupation. Without the support or help from the Pharisee, the Roman occupation would be impossible. If the Roman occupation was made more difficult, these foreigners would go home. Once this happened the people could regain control of the Temple, expel the High Priest and the King. Zadok was not sure where Ahmed was getting his assessment and it did not matter. Zadok trusted the assessment as he was trained to do. Ahmed, Zadok, nor those making the assessments had any idea as to what full Roman suppression was really like. Sadly that would change.

As it was the case so often with Ahmed he jumped around when explaining things. Zadok was accustomed to this practice of his and did not interrupt. Zadok would put the pieces together later after Ahmed told him who they were going to kill. If he had any questions he would ask Ahmed at that time. Naturally, Zadok assumed that the fact the Ahmed was present. Someone or two, maybe more, people were going to die.

Ahmed asked Zadok to recall the time when shortly after he began training him. Ahmed returned with Aaron critically injured. Clearly, there was no need to wait for a reply. Ahmed said that the business trip was a set up. This was a bit surprising to Zadok. Any business trip his father attended was arranged by either his father or Uncle Shem. Someone wanted Aaron dead. With this Zadok set back in his chair for the first time and looked around the room inspecting it.

As Ahmed continued he indicated that he had learned through his network of Spotters something rather surprising about Zadok's Great Uncle Shem. Shem was Zadok's grandfather's younger brother. It was Zadok's grandfather and great grandfather that started the carpet trading business in the city as a cover for their other activities. They placed Shem nominally in charge of the business.

Shem, over the years, had repeated ongoing communication with a priest of sorts named Jbezan in Damascus. Almost without exception whenever there was a correspondence sent from Shem to Jbezan in Damascus, a series of correspondences were generated that ultimately landed in the lap of the High Priest in the City of David. That is why Ahmed was now in the city of David.

Their network of Spotters did not reach into the City of David. At least not yet anyway, Murad and Luqman were working hard to train candidates. However, the Ebonites had people in the City of David and the surrounds. Zadok thought for a moment and then began with his questions.

Ahmed continued by asking Zadok to recall his first mission, specifically the place where Zadok killed the broker. There were a number of artifacts found after the fire that belonged to cousins of Zadok. The Spotters of theirs that inspected the artifacts also found artifacts belonging to the House of Judah. This sent Zadok's head spinning. What were artifacts belonging to the House of Judah doing so far away from Palestine.

Ahmed indicated that he and his people have been preoccupied with answering that question for the last thirteen years. He has found his answer there in the City of David. The answer has placed the House of Joseph in the greatest danger than it has ever been. Unfortunately, the danger also applied to the Ebonites. Zadok dropped his head and closed his eyes and slumped back into his chair. Ahmed took this as a sign that Zadok could take no more. He paused while staring at Zadok looking for a sign when he could continue. Ahmed was nowhere near finished.

About the Author

Woodrow Manning Jr. aka M. Bilal Hook was born and raised in Philadelphia Pennsylvania. He was educated in the Philadelphia Public School System. After which he attended Cheyney University where he earned a B.A. in Chemistry. He worked in the chemical and plastics industries for 10 years before setting out on his own as an entrepreneur.

Throughout this entire period of time he has had a fascination with history, in particular world history and religious history. After retiring he decided to write a series of novels part history and part fiction to bring his passion to the public. The "Messiah?" is the first of these Novels. He hopes you enjoy reading these books as much as he has enjoyed researching and writing them.

"The Messiah?"

This is not the story you think you know...

By A.B. Naas

As Told to Woodrow Manning Jr.
Volume 1

www.ingramcontent.com/pod-product-compliance
Lightning Source LLC
Chambersburg PA
CBHW070929130626
46555CB00001B/350